# WHAT'S NEXT?

# WHAT'S NEXT?

**JOHN PUGH JR.**

*with* **CHIP WOMICK**

*100 Years of Inspired Living
By A Man With An Unseen Handicap*

TATE PUBLISHING
AND ENTERPRISES, LLC

*What's Next?*
Copyright © 2015 by John Pugh Jr. with Chip Womick. All rights reserved.

No part of this publication may be reproduced, stored in a retrieval system or transmitted in any way by any means, electronic, mechanical, photocopy, recording or otherwise without the prior permission of the author except as provided by USA copyright law.

This book is designed to provide accurate and authoritative information with regard to the subject matter covered. This information is given with the understanding that neither the author nor Tate Publishing, LLC is engaged in rendering legal, professional advice. Since the details of your situation are fact dependent, you should additionally seek the services of a competent professional.

The opinions expressed by the author are not necessarily those of Tate Publishing, LLC.

Published by Tate Publishing & Enterprises, LLC
127 E. Trade Center Terrace | Mustang, Oklahoma 73064 USA
1.888.361.9473 | www.tatepublishing.com

Tate Publishing is committed to excellence in the publishing industry. The company reflects the philosophy established by the founders, based on Psalm 68:11,
*"The Lord gave the word and great was the company of those who published it."*

Book design copyright © 2015 by Tate Publishing, LLC. All rights reserved.
*Cover design by Jan Sunday Quilaquil*
*Interior design by Jimmy Sevilleno*

Published in the United States of America
ISBN: 978-1-63063-976-1
Biography & Autobiography / General
14.11.12

*To my children and grandchildren,
to my friends and neighbors,
and to all the people out there
who believe in the spirit of man,
the spirit of God,
the spirit of the son, Jesus,
and the Holy Spirit.*

# Contents

Preface . . . . . . . . . . . . . . . . . . . . . . . . . . . . . . . . 9
My Confession Of Faith. . . . . . . . . . . . . . . . . . . . . 11
After My Confession Of Faith . . . . . . . . . . . . . . . . . 13
An Unlikely Future. . . . . . . . . . . . . . . . . . . . . . . . 15
You're Not Paying Attention. . . . . . . . . . . . . . . . . . 19
First Job And A New Family . . . . . . . . . . . . . . . . . 23
Making A House A Home. . . . . . . . . . . . . . . . . . . 27
A New Lease On Life . . . . . . . . . . . . . . . . . . . . . . 31
A High-Risk Dream. . . . . . . . . . . . . . . . . . . . . . . 35
Service Equals Success . . . . . . . . . . . . . . . . . . . . . 39
A Gas Price 'War'. . . . . . . . . . . . . . . . . . . . . . . . . 41
Change Is Good For Business . . . . . . . . . . . . . . . . 45
'Just Plain Old Staying With It' . . . . . . . . . . . . . . . 49
In Expansion Mode . . . . . . . . . . . . . . . . . . . . . . . 53
The Flying Bug. . . . . . . . . . . . . . . . . . . . . . . . . . 55
Building Pugh Field . . . . . . . . . . . . . . . . . . . . . . . 59
One Happy 'Customer'. . . . . . . . . . . . . . . . . . . . . 65
The Ups And Downs Of Flying . . . . . . . . . . . . . . . 67
A New Venture. . . . . . . . . . . . . . . . . . . . . . . . . . 79

North To Alaska . . . . . . . . . . . . . . . . . . . . . . . . . . . . . 83
Back To The Land. . . . . . . . . . . . . . . . . . . . . . . . . . . . 87
Here Come The Cows . . . . . . . . . . . . . . . . . . . . . . . . 91
A Boyhood Dream Come True. . . . . . . . . . . . . . . . . 95
Another Northern Excursion . . . . . . . . . . . . . . . . . . 99
Out Of A Job . . . . . . . . . . . . . . . . . . . . . . . . . . . . . . 103
Home Sweet Home . . . . . . . . . . . . . . . . . . . . . . . . . 105
Lessons In Healthy Living . . . . . . . . . . . . . . . . . . . . 107
Move It, Move It, Move It . . . . . . . . . . . . . . . . . . . . 111
My Beloved . . . . . . . . . . . . . . . . . . . . . . . . . . . . . . . 115
O Canada! . . . . . . . . . . . . . . . . . . . . . . . . . . . . . . . . 117
The Games Go On. . . . . . . . . . . . . . . . . . . . . . . . . . 121
A Forbidding But Beautiful Place. . . . . . . . . . . . . . . 123
The Oldest Visitor . . . . . . . . . . . . . . . . . . . . . . . . . . 127
A Flight Of Honor. . . . . . . . . . . . . . . . . . . . . . . . . . 131
On The Dance Floor In Maui. . . . . . . . . . . . . . . . . . 135
A Minor Bump In The Road . . . . . . . . . . . . . . . . . . 141
Remembering North Carolina Veterans . . . . . . . . . . 143
A Nightmare Of Infections . . . . . . . . . . . . . . . . . . . 145
Back In The Games . . . . . . . . . . . . . . . . . . . . . . . . . 149
Ditching The Drugs . . . . . . . . . . . . . . . . . . . . . . . . . 151
The Games Beckon. . . . . . . . . . . . . . . . . . . . . . . . . . 155
At The Games. . . . . . . . . . . . . . . . . . . . . . . . . . . . . . 157
Bringing Home The Gold. . . . . . . . . . . . . . . . . . . . . 159
A New Role: Spectator . . . . . . . . . . . . . . . . . . . . . . . 161
Goodbye To Cleveland . . . . . . . . . . . . . . . . . . . . . . . 165
Back In The Groove . . . . . . . . . . . . . . . . . . . . . . . . . 169
Good For Five More Years . . . . . . . . . . . . . . . . . . . . 171
A Century…And Counting . . . . . . . . . . . . . . . . . . . 173
Dancing With The Randolph Stars . . . . . . . . . . . . . 175
My Search For Knowledge . . . . . . . . . . . . . . . . . . . . 179

# Preface

THIS IS THE true personal story of a hundred-year-old man who was born with an invisible and unknown handicap.

It tells how he overcame most of the daily problems he faced during his long life on earth.

He gives credit to his family, friends, and neighbors for much help along the way. The majority of the credit he gives to the inspiration from his spirit and motivation from his faith.

# My Confession of Faith

I AM A born-again Christian.

In August 1929, at the age of sixteen, I went to the altar of Pleasant Cross Christian Church, my home church, and got down on my knees. I asked for forgiveness of my sins and made a confession of faith in Almighty God and the Holy Spirit.

That night, an emotional feeling came over me like no other ever has.

My God is my merciful Heavenly Father. In my prayers, I address him as such. My personal relationship is on a daily spiritual basis.

The Gospel of St. John, chapter 4, verse 24, tells me that God is a Spirit; and they that worship him must worship him in spirit and in truth. Another scripture that has helped me through a long life on Earth is found in the book of Isaiah, chapter 41, verse 10: "Fear thou not, for I am with thee, be not dismayed, for I am thy God, I will strengthen thee, yea, I will help thee, yea, I will uphold thee with the right hand of my righteousness."

My God tells me that he has given me the right to make choices—and that I will be held responsible and accountable for those choices. My God tells me I was born a sinner and I must make a choice about what I am going to do about it.

I have spent a lot of hours of my life reading inspirational books. The Holy Bible is superior to them all. Mine is old and well worn and shows the effects of much use over a long period of time.

I have lived a long and eventful life on Earth. I have had my moments of stress, doubts and uncertainties. I know that I have had help from my neighbors on earth – and my God in heaven—to keep me moving.

I did not have the talents needed for leadership roles, but I have been able to help others in many different ways. For these opportunities, I am very thankful.

In 1929, I got on my knees before the altar of God as a repentant sinner. As long as I live on the earth, I will still be a repentant sinner.

# After My Confession of Faith

IN THE BEGINNING after my confession of faith, I did not clearly understand the meaning of being born again. I did not fully comprehend that my faith and the Holy Spirit were a spiritual birth and were the components of my future spiritual life—something that I did not have at my natural birth.

In my new spiritual birth, I would have to learn and grow through time and experience in my ability to fully understand that my faith and the Holy Spirit were a divine guiding force in my life on earth. I had to realize that it was up to me to choose to listen and obey.

As the days went by and I became more involved in solving the problems of my earthly life and became more dependent on guidance from my spiritual life, I became stronger in my personal spirit and my faith.

My confidence to make good decisions in whatever venture I undertook continued to grow. Having good relationships with the people around me was also a part of my daily progress. I was thankful for the opportunities that had come my way. My enjoyment in my endeavors and the rewards they brought were satisfying.

I was able to travel with my family to different parts of our great country. Being able to own some fulfilled my love of the land. Being able to travel and visit many natural wonders fulfilled my love of nature.

As I am nearing a century on earth, I can look back over my life with humble thanksgiving for the privilege of being born again.

*The main thing was desire—the wanting to. To me, life is what you make it to a great extent. Not a hundred percent, but it's how you adapt to circumstances. Everything I've done, anybody else could do if they had the desire or the will.*

# An Unlikely Future

I WAS A barefoot boy of twelve when I saw my first plane.

The World War I–era biplane was soaring through the Carolina sky over my father's farm while I was out in the tobacco field chopping weeds.

I was alone, so I stopped to watch, mesmerized as the plane flew past, growing smaller and smaller until it disappeared in the distance.

I do not recall what thoughts rumbled through my head as I leaned on my hoe and that wondrous plane sputtered through the air. I do know that I had never seen anything like it. It might as well have been from the stars.

Fewer than ten years had gone by since I'd encountered a motor vehicle for the first time, another memory that's been forever etched into my mind.

We lived in a little cotton mill village called White Oak, just a stone's throw from Greensboro, North Carolina, in Guilford County, the virtual center of the Old North State's ever-expanding textile universe of the day.

I was playing in the front yard of the small factory house my father rented from Cone Mills—the house where I was born—when a commotion down the street caught my attention.

I looked up and saw a contraption rolling my way that I can still picture today. The strange-looking vehicle—I know now that it was a Model T Ford pickup truck—had no top, just a windshield, a front seat and a driver holding onto a steering wheel. The back end was nothing more than a flat wooden bed and it was packed with wild people.

They passed me, ringing bells and shouting, "The war is over! The war is over!"

I was five when World War I, the Great War, ended in November of 1918. I'm sure my mouth hung open and my eyes grew wide as saucers. The corner of the world I inhabited was home to creaking wagons and little buggies pulled by sweating horses and stubborn mules.

I never could have envisioned a future that would find me at an intersection on a little two-lane blacktop less than thirty miles from where I saw that strange truck—and where I would start a successful business dedicated to keeping cars and trucks on the road.

But, even more unlikely, I could never have dreamed of a future in which I would build a long, narrow runway on a hillside next to that rural highway—just miles from where I saw that biplane as a boy—and that I would pilot my own airplanes into the sky from that grassy strip.

I could not have imagined these things because how many children in those early days of the twentieth century even knew such possibilities existed?

The fact that I would one day accomplish those things—and more—seems more outlandish in light of a basic truth.

I was born with an invisible handicap.

I cannot hear very well.

If you are standing right behind me and speak to me in a normal tone of voice, I probably will not hear what you say.

But, hard as it is to imagine, I did not realize I had a handicap until I was 34 and had already served two years in the U.S. Army Air Force during World War II.

*I can't hear no better today than the day I was born.
I can deal with it better.*

# You're Not Paying Attention

MY DAD AND my namesake, John Quincy Pugh, moved the family to a small farm in Randolph County, North Carolina, in 1919, near another little mill town named Franklinville.

My father was from Randolph County. He grew up on a farm. My mother, Alice Davidson Pugh, was raised in a crossroads community in Stokes County called Dillard. Her father was a blacksmith.

The promise of work brought them both to Cone Mills; him from the south, her from the west. My dad found work as a butcher in the company store. He was also employed on the company farm where cattle were raised and slaughtered for sale in the store. The store, which stocked most everything a mill worker might need to keep a household, had a clothing section. My mother was a seamstress in that department.

She was the architect of the move. She wanted a place in the country where we would have space to tend a garden and plant fruit trees, a place to keep chickens and a milk cow. We would be more self-sufficient and better able to provide for a growing family, which included my two sisters and me.

Dad agreed, but in the beginning, he kept his company job—the primary source of income—and just came home on weekends.

I was due to turn six that fall and start school. My mother took me to see the village doctor to make sure I was ready. She suspected there might be something wrong with me.

I spent most of my time in the woods by myself, climbing trees, watching birds build nests, wading in creeks and trying to catch eels and minnows, and enjoying a thousand other things, drinking in all the marvels of the natural world.

I was nature's barefoot boy, bright and eager to learn.

But what my mother and others observed was a lad who sometimes did not listen to what they were saying, or worse, ignored them.

The doctor checked my hearing.

He peered into my ears and announced that they appeared to be fine. He thumped a tuning fork on a table and asked me to let him know when I heard the sound. After repeating the tapping procedure a few times and gauging my responses, he turned to my mother.

"I don't think he has a hearing problem," the doctor pronounced. "He may have an attention problem."

For a long time after that, I was branded as a boy who did not pay attention.

Even so, my school days started well. My first-grade teacher spent a lot of one-on-one time with her students.

I learned to color pictures, mastered the ABCs, and took the first steps in learning to read and write. I enjoyed the first year.

Things began to go downhill the second year. I continued to excel in reading and writing. Things that I could see, I could understand and I could do. But whenever the teacher stood in front of the class and talked—presenting a lesson or giving instructions—I had trouble. And I had trouble because, while I could hear (I am not deaf) I could not hear well enough in many situations to understand my mom, or the lesson or the instructions.

But I did not know that.

No one, at home or at school, ever told me that I was hard of hearing.

What I did hear, over and over and over, was this: "You're not paying attention."

As I advanced into the higher grades, I earned good marks in many subjects. I loved history and geography and did well in them. If I could read and study something on my own, I learned pretty easily. If I had to rely on hearing what a teacher was saying to learn something, I was lost.

The "he does not listen" label followed me throughout my school days. I got tired of hearing it. I was miserable in school and wanted out.

I was fifteen and in the ninth grade when I asked my father to sign for me to drop out of school and go to work in a hosiery mill a few miles away in the town of Asheboro.

I never did think I was stupid, but I thought I was lacking in something.

*In my younger days, I worked all day and sat up reading into the wee hours of the morning. I learned a lot that way.*

# First Job and a New Family

THE HOSIERY BUSINESS was blossoming in Asheboro—and on the verge of booming—when I took my first public job in one of the city's textile mills in 1928.

I was fortunate enough to land a position learning to run a knitting machine that produced full-fashion hosiery for women—stockings with seams that were shaped to the contour of the leg. They were all the rage until the 1950s and 1960s.

Full-fashion knitters earned the highest wages on the factory floor, but as a trainee, I was paid just ten cents an hour. I put in ten-hour days during the week to earn a dollar a day and received fifty cents for working Saturday mornings. I paid a quarter a day to catch a ride to and from work.

I did not get my own knitting machine—and the production wages that went with it—for almost two years. But my dad had moved to Randolph County by then, giving up his job in the company store. I was the only member of the family with a paying job, so I gave most of the money I made to my father to help make ends meet.

Soon after turning eighteen, I bought a second-hand Ford. I no longer had to pay for a ride to work—which immediately boosted my net earnings. Soon, I also had people paying for rides in my car—another pay hike. I started giving my mom weekly room and board for living at home, but still had money left over. I traded my used car for a new one the following year.

During this period in my life, I had time to do something I still love to do: Read.

I'm not much interested in fantasy and fiction—I could probably count the number of novels I've read on one hand—but I am enamored with books on history, nature, and geography, and I am fascinated by biographies.

It never has taken much sleep to keep me going, which proved beneficial in the years when I established and built my own business enterprises. Often I read late into the night, engrossed in the ancient past, or the topography of a country on the other side of the world, or the life, times, and accomplishments of a famous individual. During those late hours, I slowly began building, book by finished book, a storehouse of knowledge that would come in handy down the road.

For a couple of years, I met and dated a succession of nice girls. My social life suddenly changed in October of my twentieth year when I went out with a girl named Maxine Hill. Her daddy was Virgil Hill, who had a farm on Caraway Creek in western Randolph County. She was sixteen.

It was a blind date and we hit it off from the start. She never showed any sign of concern about my hearing problem. In fact, it's an odd thing, but after I quit school and joined the workaday world, no one ever mentioned my disability. They just seemed to accept it.

Maxine and I dated steadily for several months before heading down to South Carolina to get married in April of 1934. I had little money and my assets were limited—a car and a good job. She was working in a hosiery mill too.

We decided that we would board with my parents since they had plenty of room. That did not last long. A couple of months later, we learned that Maxine was pregnant. The situation called for a new game plan. We rented a three-room apartment in Asheboro and bought furniture on credit.

I traded my car as a down payment on the next year's model. The transaction would leave us without transportation for about a year, but it would save the costs of operating a car. Besides, we lived within walking distance of work, the grocery store, and the post office.

Before long, I had a chance to rent a new house. It was larger than the apartment (it had four rooms) and cost less. The only drawback was location as it was out of town. I went back to the car dealer and did some dickering. He agreed to let me have a new car sooner than originally scheduled. So we moved to the new house.

Our first son, Richard, was born there on March 8, 1935.

On building a house: *I figured I could do it and I did. It really was my first real venture, so to speak. The thing about it, I couldn't build what I wanted, so I built what I could.*

## Making a House a Home

MY JOB IN the Asheboro hosiery mill was on the graveyard shift. For years, the nighttime schedule suited our little family, or at least we adapted to it. But when I got a first-shift job offer from a new hosiery mill in Burlington, North Carolina, I took it.

I would be operating a spanking new machine there, and they offered Maxine a day job to boot.

We liked the company and the people but did not want to settle down in Alamance County. It was adjacent to Randolph, but it was not home. When we were offered jobs two years later in another new mill, we came "home." This factory was in the Randolph County town of Randleman. We moved there.

In those days, it was several miles north of Asheboro. Today, the cities share a common boundary. You drive out of one and you're in the other.

I bought six acres on Highway 64, a few miles east of Asheboro. Tired of paying rent, I planned to build our dream house on the property.

My vision was bigger than what we could afford to finance. But I was determined. I scaled back my plans. A smaller house would still hold all the furniture we owned. And, I reasoned, I could build it myself, buying materials as I went along. Never mind that I knew nothing about building a house: I ordered a set of books that detailed house construction from start to finish.

Then I asked to switch to third shift, so I could work in the hosiery mill by night and work on the house by day.

I could write a book about the year I spent building that house. I figure I experienced just about every emotion known to man. The entire process was one of trial and error—much trial and many errors. I felt frustration due to my inexperience and ignorance of basic building skills. I felt despair at having to do things a second time that I thought I had done right the first time. I felt pain, bruises, and not a little bit of anger whenever I hammered my thumb or a piece of lumber I'd dropped bounced off my bony shins.

But I could not quit.

I would not quit.

First, I dug a foundation and laid the brick. Then I went to Seagrove Lumber Company and told Frank Auman, who owned the place, that I wanted to buy one pickup truck load of materials at a time from him, as I needed them. That was fine with Mr. Auman.

My first load was the lumber to build the framework. It was slow work, but I finally finished it. And it stood up on its own. Next came the doors and window frames; the rafters, the wood sheeting for the roof, and the asphalt shingles; then the siding, the windows, the flooring, and the ceilings.

I chose tongue-and-groove lumber for the ceilings and planned to use the same thing for the interior walls. Mr. Auman suggested that I could save a lot of money by using rough, culled lumber to make the walls and then cover them with wallpaper instead of painting them.

I needed to save money wherever I could, so I took his advice. I had no idea what I was getting into. Learning to hang wallpaper was a humbling experience.

Tacking cheesecloth onto the walls was simple enough. Brushing sizing onto the cheesecloth so it would stick to the walls was no problem either. The problem occurred with the third step in the process, mixing a paste of water and flour, brushing it onto the wallpaper and sticking the paper to the wall.

The first two pieces of wallpaper hung beautifully. The third was a disaster. Apparently I had gotten the proper amount of paste on the first two pieces of paper by sheer luck. If I applied too much paste, the wallpaper would tear when I tried to hang it and move it into position. If I used too little, the paper would not stick.

I ruined a lot of wallpaper before I got the hang of it. But I did get the hang of it. I added a pretty paper border around the top of the walls to complete the interior decorating.

Finally, I installed the doors, finished painting, and built two sets of steps, one for the front door, one for the back.

When I was done, I stepped back and admired what I had created. And I experienced a final emotion: I loved that house.

I had spent all of 1939 working on it, sleeping just a few hours every night before heading off to the mill. We moved into our new home, which had two bedrooms with a large closet between them, a kitchen-dining room combination, and a sitting room.

The house was paid for. My renting days were over.

*A lot of human beings have done a lot for me—everybody that I've ever had for a friend or a neighbor. We don't travel this world alone. If we're successful, we have to have help from our friends and our neighbors.*

# A New Lease on Life

IN 1943, TWO years after the United States entered the fray of World War II, I decided to volunteer to serve my country. It was something I had wanted to do for some time.

I knew that the armed forces accepted married men, but I was concerned that they might not accept me because of my hearing problem.

My family and friends were shocked.

I heard a similar refrain time and again: "You know they won't have you."

That made me even more determined.

I recalled the long-ago trip to the doctor who had found nothing wrong when he peered into my ears and tapped the tuning fork before I started school. I surmised that if I did not tell anyone I had trouble hearing, they would not discover it during an exam.

And I was right.

I traveled to the induction center at Camp Croft, South Carolina, for a physical. The hearing test was last on the list. I passed everything else with flying colors.

The sergeant doing the exam stood close to me, whispered in my ear, and said, "Repeat after me."

When he whispered, I whispered.

And he passed me.

My family could not believe it when I returned home and told them I was now a member of the U.S. armed forces and would be leaving for basic training in a few days.

Basic training in Atlantic City, New Jersey, was uneventful, and so was my advanced training in ordnance school on the banks of the Mississippi River in Savannah, Illinois.

My hearing problem nearly caught up with me at my first duty after I arrived at the Salt Lake City disbursement center to receive my duty assignment.

For ten days, I made roll call every morning.

I never heard my name called.

Finally, in frustration, I headed to headquarters. There was a sergeant behind the desk.

"I want to know when in the hell I'm going to get out of this godforsaken place," I said.

He asked for my name and looked it up.

"Where in hell have you been?" he asked. "You've been AWOL for ten days."

I told him I had not been AWOL, I had been busy doing KP and picking up cigarette butts on the grounds for the past ten days. The next morning I was on a train bound for Pocatello Army Air Base in Idaho, where I spent fourteen months in the ordnance office.

I was a sergeant, responsible for keeping track of all the ordnance equipment on the base. When Germany surrendered in May of 1945, the air base was closed.

Auditors checked all the records first. My department was the first one cleared on the base. My commanding officer, Captain Harper, received a letter of commendation from Army Air Force headquarters—and Captain Harper gave one to me.

Both of us were sent to Fort Sumner air base in New Mexico to await reassignment. While we were there, Captain Harper set the wheels in motion on something that changed my life.

"John," he said to me one day, "this war is going to be over soon. I think it would be a good idea for me to get you transferred to an Army hospital for servicemen with hearing disabilities to see if they can help you."

I agreed with him.

And that is how I wound up at an Army hospital in Chickasha, Oklahoma, where a doctor examined me with special equipment.

Then he explained why I had trouble hearing. He told me I had a unique condition: I had been born with fixed eardrums. They did not vibrate like normal eardrums when sound waves hit them.

The condition did not prevent me from hearing, but it meant that I could only hear one frequency clearly. The doctor said I had 40 percent hearing in my left ear and 60 percent in the right.

He said no operation could repair the condition. Hearing aids could help me hear sounds better, but they probably would not help me understand what I was hearing. He suggested I learn lip reading and sent me to a class.

After the first session, the teacher called me aside and told me I did not need to come back.

"Why?" I asked.

"You read lips better than I do," she said.

I had learned to read lips on my own, without knowing it.

Finding out the true nature of my handicap was monumental.

It changed me, but it also changed the way people treated me. Before, there was no visible sign of my disability. Now there was. I came home from the service wearing a hearing aid in each ear.

People were kinder, more understanding.

Most, it seemed, wanted to help me any way they could.

I owed credit to Captain Harper for my new lease on life. A few years after the war, I drove to his home in Missouri and told him so.

*I wanted to live beyond a job in a mill, not that I was unhappy or anything, but I knew I couldn't accomplish anything in the mill but living.*

# A High-Risk Dream

AFTER RETURNING HOME from the service, I headed back to the hosiery mill, but I had a dream for a different future: I wanted to start my own business and leave the mill behind forever.

It was an ambitious notion—bold might be a better word—for a fellow with my background. From the time I quit school at fifteen to take a job, I had never known anything but working inside the walls of a factory. No member of my family had ever owned, or even managed, a business. None of my friends had a smidgen of business experience. Neither did I, but that did not deter me.

I owned a small tract of land five miles east of Asheboro on Highway 64, where a little paved road intersected with the highway. The smaller road wound down to a tiny mill village named Cedar Falls, which stood on the banks of the Deep River a couple of miles away.

My grand vision was to build a service station at that rural intersection. Sell gasoline, tires, batteries, and other parts. Do minor repairs and oil changes. Wash cars.

I hired a building contractor and visited a local building and loan association. When the station was completed, I would need $4,000 to finish paying for it. The loan company manager sent me to talk to two businessmen on the company's board of directors. I was told that these men and a third man would decide how much money the association would loan me.

After hearing my plans, the men advised me that I could expect to get $4,000. My first lesson in business dealings came after the building was finished and I needed the money to finish paying for it. The building and loan men came to see the new block building. Then they announced that they would only loan me $3,500.

I had barely enough money to pay for equipment and supplies to open but I had no choice except to dip into those funds to make up for the $500 shortage.

With that unexpected development behind me, I opened the doors on my dream endeavor, Pugh Esso, in May of 1947. I hired an experienced man to cover the day shift and a man to help him. On weekdays, I planned to continue pulling my day shift at the mill and then work the night shift at the station. On Saturdays and Sundays, I planned to work both shifts at the station.

I had no business experience but knew better than to quit my factory job until I was sure the venture was profitable.

Considering my lack of experience—and the fact that the station was five miles from a town of any size—opening the business was a high-risk undertaking.

But my business sense proved to be pretty good (maybe it was just common sense) and the location proved to be a positive.

To the best of my knowledge, there were no other exclusive service stations out in the country on Highway 64 in 1947.

My little cinder block station stood in the center of North Carolina on the main highway that carried a lot of traffic to the east toward Raleigh, the state capital, and westward, to the cities of Charlotte and Asheville. A goodly amount of traffic that passed was bound for Norfolk and Richmond, cities in Virginia—and a lot of that traffic was trucks.

I realized quickly that if my business was going to make it, I needed to attract patronage from the people who regularly traveled that highway.

Other service stations in the area were in towns. They opened around seven o'clock in the morning and typically closed at about six in the afternoon. They were not open when some travelers passed by. To take advantage of this situation, I established longer hours, opening at 6:00 a.m. and closing at 11:00 p.m.

At first, just a few travelers pulled in to my station—to use the restrooms and maybe to have a Coke and pack of crackers. A few bought gas. As time passed, more and more people started stopping. And more and more began buying gas.

The station did not cover expenses in the first six months, but it did the second six months. At the end of a year, revenue was still short of expenses, but business was slowly increasing every month. As I learned what customers wanted, and were willing to buy, I adjusted the services we offered and the stock we kept on hand.

When year two ended, the station had generated a small profit and I decided to quit the mill and devote all my energies to the station. Doing this made a big difference in a short time.

My original hope was that I could build a business that would support my family. I never expected things to turn out the way they did.

But you never know if what you try will work.

And if you do not try, you will never know.

*I had an idea. Through trial and error I made it work. But what if I hadn't tried?*

# Service Equals Success

THE THIRD YEAR started out well.

Having the owner of the business always at hand to greet customers, and make sure they were treated special, was extremely productive. We built a very good local business to complement our highway trade.

I wore my hearing aids while I was working, so customers were aware of my handicap. They were kind and considerate and seemed to want to help me. The feeling was mutual.

I initiated the practice of cleaning the windshield on every car that pulled in (or had an employee do it if I was busy), whether the motorist bought fuel or just used the restroom and moved on. Soon, customers who had previously stopped only for a bathroom break or a snack break began buying gas too.

Another advantage in our favor was that we fixed flat tires and provided road service. We were the only station on Highway 64 between Charlotte and Raleigh that repaired large truck tires. Fixing flats was one of our most profitable services.

In 1947, there was no modern tire-changing equipment available in our area. We worked with handheld tire tools, rubber hammers and sledgehammers. Fixing a large truck tire was particularly risky. When inflating a repaired tire, there was an ever-present danger that the rim could fly off and cause serious injury, even death. I always wrapped a chain round the tire and rim to prevent this from happening.

Gasoline sales climbed to a record 35,000 gallons a month, and sales of goods and services kept pace. The success attracted the attention of competitors locally and from far-flung areas of the state to the east and to the west.

Then, a company built a Texaco station right across the road from mine. The new station was modern, up to date, its gleaming porcelain exterior much more stylish than my simple little building of painted concrete block.

To say that I was worried would be putting it mildly. This was big-time competition. I was certain the new kid on the block would hurt my business and I had no big company to help me.

Shortly before the new station opened, the district manager for Standard Oil in Charlotte stopped by.

"Well, Pugh," he said, "I see you're going to have some competition."

"Yes, sir," I replied. "I guess they're going to get some of my business."

I did not see a bright side.

He did, and I have never forgotten what he said.

"They will not hurt you. They will help you."

Time proved him to be right.

*I've always liked competition, even in business. A lot of people don't like competition, but it'll make you better.*

# A Gas Price "War"

My fourth year in business turned out to be amazing, but it did not begin that way.

It started with the new Texaco station opening and selling gas at four cents less per gallon than my price.

I immediately called my wholesale supplier and asked what they could do to help me meet the cheaper price. Nothing, they said. They dismissed the situation as temporary. It will not last long, they said.

Meanwhile, my customers said they could not afford to keep buying gas from me when they could drive across the road and save four cents on each gallon. They asked what I was going to do about it. I told my customers that I understood and asked for a week to come up with a plan.

It was clear that if I did not come up with a solution in a few days I was going to lose the business of a lot of customers. But I also knew I was selling more gas for my supplier than any other station in the area. My competitors knew that too. I came up with an idea based on that knowledge.

On a Monday, I hired a sign painter to paint a sign on a 4-foot-by-8-foot piece of plywood—large numbers in bright red on a white background, advertising the same price for a gallon of gas as my Texaco competitor. I asked him to wait until Friday to bring the sign to my station.

We erected the sign as close to the highway as we could.

It did not take long for it to generate attention.

We noticed some of the employees of the Texaco station gathered in their driveway, looking at the sign. The station phone started ringing with calls from competitors asking if my supplier was helping me match the Texaco price. I replied that I could not tell them anything, but suggested they call their suppliers and let them know what was going on.

Some competitors came to the station to see the sign in person. They asked if they could take pictures. I said sure.

I had waited until Friday to put up the sign for a reason. I knew that officials of the supplying companies left the office early on Fridays and that no one would be able to contact them about my price gambit until Monday.

Gas sellers were not the only ones attracted by the large sign.

So were gas buyers.

We were pumping a lot of gas, keeping old customers and picking up new ones, but I was also losing four cents profit on every gallon sold. I knew I could not continue to do business on that basis for long and survive. About two weeks is what I figured.

On Monday, as I had anticipated, my competitors began contacting their suppliers to do something. During the week, officials from my supplying company, and from other supplying companies, paid my station a visit. They took pictures, asked questions, and discussed the situation.

I got the impression that my competitors believed that since I was a high-volume station, my supplier was backing me in the price cut so I could face down the competition. I never told anyone differently.

We continued to sell more and more gas. And, as more customers bought more gas, they also bought other products.

Toward the end of the week, my supplier called me with the news that they were going to cut the price of gas they sold to me after all.

It was my first big battle against competition in the business world. It was amazing to me that it had been achieved in large part due to the efforts of my competitors.

*People ask me what college I went to, what university. I didn't finish ninth grade. I went to work. I probably couldn't even pass an entrance test to a college. But there's one thing I know – that I can lose every dollar I've got and I can survive because I know how to survive.*

# Change Is Good For Business

PRIMED TO DO battle for new business, I added a third shift and the station was now open 24/7. In the beginning, I handled the third shift so I would be able to see what was needed to make those hours of operation profitable.

At first, there was very little business. I offered free coffee to those who did stop. Most who stopped were truckers who just wanted a little break or needed a bathroom stop. After about a month, I took action based on what was happening.

I graded the area to the east of the station and installed diesel and gas pumps to serve trucks. I made it easy for truckers to pull off the highway, get to the pumps, and then drive around behind the station to get back onto the road.

Next I added two large restrooms with a shower and converted a wooden building on the property into sleeping quarters for truckers. This was during the days of segregation. I converted the two original restrooms for use by black customers. Now my station was the only one in the area with restrooms for white and black customers.

Sales continued to grow. At the end of the summer season in 1950, the combined sales of diesel and gasoline stood at 65,000 gallons per month. Only one station serviced by my supplier in the state of North Carolina was selling more fuel.

I had not taken a day off since I opened the station. I needed a vacation. Maxine was working full time and could not go with me, so I drove to Morehead City, North Carolina, alone and rented a room for a week.

I spent one day on a deep-sea fishing excursion. The rest of the time I relaxed, slept, took long walks on the beach, and pondered the past four years and how much knowledge I had gained in the world of business. I spent time in humble thankfulness for my good fortune. Then I drove home and plunged back into work.

In the fifth year, I added a couple of new ventures.

One was the delivery of home heating fuel in a thousand-gallon tank truck I purchased. The other was sales and delivery of various brands of motor oil to other service stations.

I had learned that different customers preferred different brands of oil. Naturally, customers did most of their business with stations that carried the brand of motor oil they liked.

The problem for a businessman was that in 1950, major oil companies owned (or leased) most service stations. Generally, suppliers restricted station operators from selling any brand except the company brand.

That's where we came in. The stations we sold to did not display the non-company-approved motor oils in their public sales rooms. They stored the product in back rooms, so they could offer customers a wider variety. It took time, but the motor oil venture grew.

I had done what I set out to do.

By paying attention to what my customers wanted—and by being willing to work hard, very hard—I had built a successful service station business.

*I doubt I'd have been as successful as I have been if it'd been too easy. The hard way is the best way. The easy way you don't learn too much. But you learn the hard way—you don't ever forget it.*

# "Just Plain Old Staying With It"

IN 1951, MY wife, Maxine, decided she wanted to have a second child. The following year, on July 10, our second son, Alan Virgil Pugh, was born.

Alan graduated from Eastern Randolph High School and the University of North Carolina at Chapel Hill. He entered the UNC School of Law and earned a law degree. Upon graduation, he opened a law office in Asheboro.

Also in 1951, my fifth year in business, I decided to sell my gas station. For four years, I had spent nearly all my time working with little time for my family or myself.

I contacted my supplier, Esso (Standard Oil), and told them about my plans. I wanted a private buyer for the business and a fifteen-year lease on the property, payable to me monthly. If they did not agree to my proposal, I told them, I would try to sell it to another major oil company.

The company agreed to the lease after a few weeks and also agreed to help find a buyer. By summer, the company had signed the lease and found a buyer.

The transaction did not include my home heating oil business or my motor oil delivery operation. These I planned to combine in a new business named Pugh Oil Company.

The enterprise was housed in a cinder block building with an office and warehouse constructed on land I owned near my former service station. I had two 10,000-gallon tanks installed, one for fuel oil and one for kerosene. I bought a second heating oil delivery truck and hired two men, one to work in the office and one to drive a truck. I drove the other truck.

My first full year in business was 1952. I spent one day a week delivering cases of motor oil to business customers. At the time, many of my home heating oil customers had fifty-gallon drums for storage. I offered to replace the smaller drums with 275-gallon tanks free of charge. Most accepted the offer.

This accomplished two things: it reduced the frequency with which I had to refill the tanks, and it increased the number of gallons per delivery. That increased profits. It also increased our customer base as more people heard about our services.

We were open six days a week, from seven in the morning until five in the afternoon, but we offered emergency deliveries to customers who ran out of oil after hours, whether it was at night, on Sunday, or on a holiday. A twenty-four-hour telephone answering service ensured that customers could always get in touch with us. I took care of the emergency deliveries in the early days.

I was constantly looking for ways to serve my customers better, but the company still lost money the first year. The second year, we broke even. In the third year, even though we had more customers and the business had grown, we still did not make a profit.

I was discouraged. For the first time in my life as a businessman, I questioned my ability to make the operation a paying venture.

After all, I had been working an average of sixteen hours a day, six days a week. Financially, I would have been better off if I had been putting in just eight hours a day at the mill six days a week. I seriously contemplated selling my equipment and shutting the doors on the business.

Fortunately, I had a business friend who sold storage tanks and equipment. He was much older than me and had been in business for many years. I trusted him. And he had trust in me.

He stopped by the office every month to see if I needed any equipment. When he came by on this particular day, I was wrestling with my business woes. We went to a nearby restaurant for lunch and I shared my problem. I told him I had lost confidence in my ability to get the job done.

On that day, with a few simple, but wise, words, that friend did me the greatest service of any person I have ever known.

"John," he said, "success is about 98 percent persistence."

"You mean," I asked, "just plain old staying with it?"

He said that was exactly what he meant.

So I made the decision to just plain old stay with it.

The following year, the business turned a profit and from that time forward business was better every year.

*The longer I was involved, the more sure I became of myself. I was making fewer mistakes. That's really the meat of the story. It's not a fellow buying an oil truck and going out here and working hard. Anybody can do that it they want to.*

# In Expansion Mode

THE OWNER OF a brick house on two acres east of the oil company wanted to sell to me. The place also had a large brooder house for raising chickens.

The property turned out to be perfect for a major expansion. We converted the living room of the house into space for a cashier and records clerk, where customers could pay bills or get information about their accounts; the dining room became a conference room; a bedroom, my private office. We turned another room, with an outside entrance, into a dispatcher's office.

We poured a concrete floor in the old chicken house and made it a warehouse. We had three storage tanks installed. Each one held up to 20,000 gallons and was equipped with an electric pump for unloading fuel from tanker trucks.

The company now had five tank trucks for home delivery. We were also selling and delivering gasoline to farmers and other commercial customers. We had purchased two tractor-trailer tankers to haul products from the supply terminal to our storage tanks; we were also selling tractor-trailer loads of fuel to some commercial accounts.

My oldest son, Richard, graduated from Elon College in 1957. He had a business degree and other job offers, but I wanted him to join me in my company. I told him I would match any salary offers he received. I also told him that if he stayed a certain length of time (long enough to determine if he liked the business, and if he and I could work together), I would give him stock in the company. He accepted the offer.

When the previously agreed number of years had passed, I gave him the predetermined number of shares and he became a company official.

In 1970, Pugh Oil had the opportunity to buy two other local oil companies. Each represented a major brand and had its own offices and storage facilities. We arranged the purchase.

Now we had a group of service stations that would boost the sale of gasoline and related products, and we had tripled the size of the company.

*Who can say who's able to do what?*

# The Flying Bug

I WAS SIXTEEN in 1929 when I took my first airplane ride in an open cockpit biplane. The pilot was up front and there was space for two passengers in the back seat.

From that moment, I wanted to learn to fly.

But I was told, by people who were supposed to know, that a person with a hearing problem has a poor sense of balance and cannot learn to fly a plane. I did not stop wanting to learn to fly, but I set the notion aside.

Nearly three decades later, when I was forty-four, I met a former flying instructor for the Army Air Force. The man had just moved to town and we became friends. Eventually, I told him of my desire to fly and why I never pursued it.

He told me he did not know if I could learn to fly or not but there was one way to find out. If I would rent a plane, he said, he would teach me to fly it.

A friend of mine named Lonnie York owned a farm near the town of Ramseur a few miles from where I lived. He had a landing strip on his farm and owned a J3 Cub plane that he rented for training.

So I rented the plane—it cost four dollars an hour—and my new friend started giving me flying lessons. After eight hours of instruction, he announced that I was ready to fly solo. So, I took off on my first solo flight.

After gaining some altitude I looked down at the ground. The butterflies fluttered in my stomach when I realized that I had to put the plane back on the runway all by myself. There was nothing to do but grit my teeth and head down.

The airstrip was short, just 1,800 feet long. The approach passed over high-tension power lines and the grass runway ended at the far end at a stand of trees. There was little room to maneuver. I cleared the lines and put the plane down in front of my instructor.

It was a good landing. He had me do it again. Then again. And yet again. Each time, I had a little trouble, but managed to land.

The next day I returned to the field by myself, rented the plane for an hour, and practiced taking off and landing. I corrected the problems I'd had the day earlier and was making smooth landings.

The next week, I flew solo two more times. With three hours of solo time under my belt, I was confident in my ability to fly a plane and land it.

I heard about a plane for sale in a neighboring county and drove over to look at it. The Piper PA-12 had a 115-hp engine and had room for the pilot up front and two passengers in the back.

The owner and I took a forty-five-minute flight and, strange as it may sound, I decided to buy the plane. I flew the plane to York's field, put it in a hangar, and my plane-renting days were over.

Now I had to get a license to fly my new plane.

To apply for a pilot's license, I had to have a medical certificate from a doctor, proof that I had passed a medical exam. I was pretty sure that if a doctor knew about my hearing problem, he would not pass me, but I remembered the doctor who checked my ears when I was five. He did not see, or find, anything wrong with my ears.

I made an appointment with a doctor in another town, someone who did not know me. I left my hearing aids at home on the day of the exam. I answered all of the doctor's questions by reading his lips. When he checked my ears, he did not see anything wrong.

He gave me the medical certificate I needed.

The next steps to a pilot's license were passing a written test and then a flight test. As I had in the past, I turned to the written word for help. I ordered a book about preparing for the tests and studied it for several weeks.

On the day of the exam, I flew to the airport in Winston-Salem and met the examiner. I passed the written test and then we climbed in the plane.

We flew away from the airport a short distance and the examiner directed me to do some stalls, slow flying, and other maneuvers before we headed back. As we approached, the examiner moved the throttle to half power. He told me I had an "emergency."

I maintained altitude as we approached the runway. To land, I needed to lose altitude and slow the plane. To accomplish this, I started slipping the plane sideways. When the examiner saw that I intended to try to put the plane down at half throttle, he released it and I made a normal landing.

He gave me a private pilot's license.

Some of our friends had rented a beachfront cottage at Crescent Beach on the Carolina coast. I decided to take the family—my wife and younger son, Alan—to visit them.

In those days, it was permissible to land a plane on an unoccupied beach. When we arrived over the beach house, it was low tide and the beach was empty. I landed the plane on the strand. We pulled the plane above the level of high tide and spent the night. The next afternoon, we pulled the plane back down on the beach and took off for home.

*I firmly believe the Lord has helped me, but I've had to do my part, and I think that's true of every individual. We have certain responsibilities and accountabilities.*

# Building Pugh Field

NOT MANY PEOPLE have a private landing strip in their back yard, but that was my dream.

The only available land, a strip 2,000 feet long, was not ideal. Half of the strip was a hill fifty feet higher on the north end than on the south end. Beyond the north end was a ledge of rocks and a high-tension power line. The south end ended at a busy highway.

Due to the constraints, the majority of takeoffs would start on the north end. Most of the landings would approach from the south. But I decided it was doable and hired a grading contractor to build a hundred-foot-wide airstrip.

Grading would be necessary to create a smooth transition from the hill on the northern end but I did not want to remove too much dirt: The steepness would be beneficial during takeoffs and would help slow planes during landings. I planted grass seed on the graded strip, built a hangar 700 feet from my back door, mounted a windsock and flew my plane to it from York's.

For twenty-five years, I flew off this strip—Pugh Field on aviation maps—without any problems. My wife and I could pack our bags, carry them to the plane, and take off for most anywhere we wanted to go.

During my flying career I owned four planes: The Piper PA-12; a Piper Tri-Pacer with a 160-hp engine; a Piper Comanche with a 250-hp engine, retractable landing gear, and a cruising speed of 180 mph; and a Cessna 152 with a 150-hp engine.

A life of its own

I built the landing strip, with one hangar, for my personal use, but after I started flying in and out, other local pilots wanted to base their planes there too.

So, I built seven more hangars and rented them. I also installed an underground tank and pump for aviation fuel.

On weekends, when weather was good, Pugh Field was a busy place, with the local pilots coming and going and fliers visiting from other places. Asheboro did not have an airport at this time, so pilots on business trips to the city often used Pugh Field.

Pugh Field was home base to Frank Auman's helicopter. In fact, helicopters stopped at the field often.

Three men built airplanes on the property. Ernest Craven and Jack Hayworth each built a single-seat Pitts biplane and soloed them off my airstrip; Roy Johnson built a two-seater plane with a 180-hp engine and soloed it off the field. I witnessed each solo flight.

I never had an accident at the strip, but others did. Most were visiting pilots unfamiliar with the field.

A doctor from another city landed on the north end of the field. That was a mistake. It was downhill all the way and he could not stop his plane until it slid into the bank of the highway on the south end. No one was injured.

A fellow flying a Howard four-seater with a 450-hp engine approached from the south, but he came in too high. I saw his plane bounce off the runway and flip over in front of the hangars. The only injury was to his pride.

A local doctor in a Tri-Pacer stalled over the runway and the plane was badly damaged, but no one was hurt, when it hit the ground. A local pilot in a 200-hp Mooney tried to land from the south in a strong tailwind. He did not get the plane onto the runway; the wind carrying it over the northern end of the strip where it crashed onto rocks beneath the power lines. He was not injured but the airplane was a total loss. The cause: Poor judgment.

More poor judgment

The gas pump was never locked and there was no attendant.

Pilots who needed gas pumped it, signed a ticket, and put the ticket in a box. I mailed bills and was always paid. The honor system worked.

There was only one problem with this system.

One time.

At about eleven one night, when I was ready to go to bed, a neighbor who lived next door called. He said he had seen a car drive up to the airport's gas pump. I grabbed my shotgun, jumped in my pickup and headed for the pump. There was only one way in and out of the airport.

When I arrived, there was a car backed up to the pump and the nozzle was sticking into the fuel tank. But there was no one in sight. The culprit apparently had run into the hangar when I drove up.

I parked my truck with its headlights trained on the hangar. After a few minutes two men came walking out. I pulled the gun from the bed of the truck and pointed it at them. They stopped and I asked what they were doing.

They said a friend had told them they could get gas here. I said they were lying, that they had simply come to steal gas.

When I asked their names, they told me, but said they were both on probation and did not want me to call the law. I informed them that I could handle the situation, that they were on my property, stealing from me and then lying about it.

"This gun is loaded," I said. "If you give me any trouble I won't try to kill you but I will blow your legs off and it will be a long time before you walk again."

I explained that I had the keys to their car.

"Pay me for the gas and I will let you go," I said.

They said they did not have any money.

Go get some, I said.

They asked how they were supposed to go get money. I told them to start walking.

They asked where they would find me when they returned with money. I told them I was going to be in bed sleeping and that they had better not wake me up. I said they could bring the money to my office in the morning and I would give them the keys.

When I arrived at the office the next morning, they were there with the money. I told those boys that I had been really angry the night before and I was no longer angry. But I had a message for them.

"I hate a thief and if I ever see either one of you on my property again, I will shoot you."

They had to walk a short distance to their car and I saw them leave a few minutes later. If either of them has ever set foot on my property again, I am not aware of it.

*Creating things motivates me. I like to try something new.
I think a lot of time we create our own enjoyment
to life by how we approach it.*

# One Happy 'Customer'

I LOGGED OVER two thousand hours in the air, including many cross-country flights and many trips for business. But the flying I enjoyed most was the time I spent taking friends and neighbors (especially children) on their first flights over our beautiful countryside.

I never charged anyone a penny and I only took people up for first flights when the weather was good and the air smooth. I tried to make all the climbs, turns and descents as smooth as possible. I didn't want my passengers to be uneasy.

I wanted everyone to love flying as I did—and I was routinely rewarded with smiles and with how many wanted to go flying again.

My wife's sister lived across the highway from my landing strip and she had a five-year-old boy named Frank.

I took Frank up in the Comanche for his first flight.

He loved it.

Every time he saw me getting the plane out of the hangar after that he came running and shouting, "Uncle John, wait for me!"

He loved flying so much that I took him up every opportunity I could. One day when we were flying alone, I put the plane on automatic pilot. Of course, he did not know that.

I asked if he wanted to fly the plane. He looked at me wide-eyed, wondering if I meant it. I told him to take hold of the wheel and fly the plane. So he did.

The look on his little face was priceless. The autopilot moved the wheel slightly from time to time. When it did, he looked at me, as if to say, "Is everything OKAY?" I told him he was doing fine.

To this day, I cannot say who most enjoyed those moments 2,500 feet in the air at 180 mph. Was it the sixty-five-year-old pilot or the five-year-old copilot?

I do know this. That boy grew up loving and flying planes. In high school, his aviation class built a small airplane and he took it on the first test flight. After high school, he enrolled in aviation school, where he earned an aviation mechanic license, a private pilot's license, a commercial pilot's license, and a flying instructor's license.

After several jobs in the aviation field, he became a pilot for Piedmont Airlines, which was later sold to US Air. For the past several years, Frank has been flying large airliners to Europe.

Uncle John sure is proud of him.

Chalk one up to the effect of inspiration on a five-year-old's future.

*If you're prepared for what you're fixing to do,
if you get into a problem, you've already done your homework.
You know what the consequences are because you've studied
what other people did in similar circumstances.*

# The Ups and Downs of Flying

### A risky take-off

ONE OF MY brothers-in-law and a neighbor asked me to fly them to the coast where some friends were on a fishing trip. The idea was that we would land on the beach, spend the night, and come home the next day.

I did not have much flying experience at the time. The weather was fine at home so I agreed. I had no idea what kind of risk I was taking. But I found out.

The trip to Drum Inlet was uneventful. I landed the plane on the beach behind the fishermen as planned. They were in the ocean, surf fishing.

We pulled the plane higher on the shore, next to a fishing hut, where we spent the night. The next morning, we saw a thunderstorm over the water and headed our way. The tide was high and a strong wind was blowing inland from the sea. There was no way to take off from the beach, where we had come in.

Since we had no ropes or stakes to secure the plane, I knew that if the storm reached the shore it would be blown away. It was a predicament.

Though the water was high on the shore, there was still a few feet of packed sand between the plane, softer sand, and the ocean. I decided to try to take off in that little space.

I found a twenty-foot length of 2×8 timber under the hut and placed it under the plane, with the plane's tail wheel on the end of the board. I calculated that the wheel would ride the plank as I guided it toward the sea and that the strong wind blowing in would help lift the plane up over soft sand and the water.

I also figured on trying this risky takeoff alone.

But my traveling companions were intent on going.

They had no idea of the hazard involved and I did not tell them.

We got into the plane and buckled up. I let the engine warm up, put my foot on the brake, pulled the throttle wide open, and released the brake. The plane shot forward. Just before we reached the soft sand I pulled back on the control and we headed seaward, a few feet over the water. I continued on that path, slowly gaining altitude, until it was safe to make a slow turn and head back toward land. We passed the fishermen by the hut and headed for home.

There were several witnesses, but I was probably the only one who knew that just a few feet separated success and disaster on the takeoff. There is no doubt that we had a divine copilot that day.

## My first cross-country flight

On Christmas morning 1957, I decided to make my first cross-country flight to visit an old Army buddy who lived in Westernport, Maryland, on the Potomac River.

Since the Piper PA-12 did not have a radio, I would navigate using aviation maps, the plane's compass and a wristwatch. The process was fairly simple: I drew a straight line on the map from my airstrip to a small landing field near my destination. I put marks along the straight line that indicated where I expected to be every fifteen minutes during the flight.

All I needed to do was check the map at fifteen-minute intervals and then look down. If what I saw below did not match the map, I would make adjustments to get back on track.

The method worked perfectly except for one thing. I arrived over my destination on time, but the ground was covered in fog. I flew another twenty-five miles to another airport where there was no fog. I landed and waited about an hour. When the fog lifted, I returned to my original destination.

I spent most of the day with my friend then headed home. I took off from the small strip in the valley and started circling the area to gain altitude to fly over the mountains in West Virginia. I estimated my arrival back in Randolph County at 5:30 p.m., a few minutes before dark. That's when I arrived. Minutes later darkness fell.

I had completed my first cross-country trip over mountains and returned safely. I flew this plane without a radio for three years, and then traded it for the Piper Tri-Pacer, which had one.

## Going down in Cape Cod fog

In August 1962, I took off on the longest trip I'd ever taken in my flying career—to the Hyannis airport on Cape Cod in Massachusetts.

I took off at 8:00 a.m. from my Randolph County landing strip in my Piper Tri-Pacer and expected to land in Hyannis around 3:00 p.m. I was on schedule for the first couple of hours before encountering storms. I had to land and wait each storm out before continuing the journey. Flying around the storms was not a real option due to my limited navigational skills. I needed to stick to my pre-planned course or else I might have found myself in serious trouble.

The situation grew more critical with every storm and every delay, but I landed in Plymouth, Massachusetts, at six o'clock and the weather prediction for Cape Cod was clear. So I took off again, expecting to arrive at Hyannis before dark.

When I arrived, however, fog shrouded the entire cape. I was flying above the fog and was certain that I was near the airport. But I could not make radio contact.

Cape Cod is a narrow strip of land jutting into the Atlantic Ocean. I began circling the cape, looking for a hole in the fog. I made sure to stay over land because if I had to make a forced landing, I did not want it to be in the sea.

As daylight dwindled, I had to make a decision shortly. I was getting glimpses of houses, streets, and woods through the fog. I decided to land in those trees, so I would not hit any houses, if I did not find a clearing soon.

Then, there it was, a small hole through the fog with a patch of precious green earth below it. The fog was swirling.

The next time I saw the clearing through the opening, I cut the power on the plane—to avoid damage when I landed—and pointed the nose toward the ground.

I saw a house on the right, trees on the left, and a small clearing in front of me. Just before touchdown, I pulled the nose up. The plane rolled through weeds for several hundred feet before I was forced to let the nose down to avoid crashing into a stand of trees. The Piper traveled another seventy feet before the nose wheel collapsed, pitching the plane onto its nose. But it did not flip.

I climbed out and was standing a few feet from the wreckage when a police car, a fire truck, and several people arrived. A man asked if I was all right. I told him I was.

"Are you scared?" he asked.

"Not now," I replied, "but you can bet I have been."

It was ten miles to the airport. I had been close, but not close enough. I had landed on a small farm owned by Mr. and Mrs. Crow. I never did ask them their first names. They invited me to spend the night and Mrs. Crow prepared food. We talked after eating and then made ready for bed. She asked if I need something to help me sleep. I thanked her, but explained that I was so thankful to be alive that I would have no trouble sleeping.

The next morning, Mrs. Crow drove me to the Hyannis airport to make arrangements to have my plane stored until I could send a truck from Asheboro to pick it up. I tried to pay Mrs. Crow for her kindnesses, but she refused. I will never forget this wonderful, caring Cape Cod couple for their assistance in my hour of need.

I bought a one-way ticket home and left Cape Cod a sadder, wiser, and more humble person than I had been when I left home.

## New wheels (and wings)

The Piper was trucked to a Randolph County facility for repair. The nose wheel was broken and the propeller was bent, but there was no major damage. I flew the plane for a couple more years before trading it for a Piper Comanche 250.

This four-seater airplane was larger and faster and boasted more bells and whistles, including retractable landing gear. I used the plane for several business trips; my wife and I made several trips to Cape Cod and Florida and frequently flew to Kitty Hawk on North Carolina's Outer Banks and to South Carolina's Crescent Beach.

During trips to Cape Cod, I always flew over the ocean from Red Bank, New Jersey, to lower Long Island to avoid flying over New York City. On one of those trips with my wife, Maxine, and younger son, Alan, along, we ran into bad weather over Long Island and had to turn around.

As we were flying back, I saw an airliner emerge from the haze along the coast and knew that a major airport was nearby. I called air traffic control and explained our situation. We needed a place to land.

They asked where we were. I told them we were over the Atlantic, flying in clear weather and that I estimated we were about fourteen miles offshore. They asked me to do a couple of maneuvers so they could identify my plane on radar. They radioed that we were eleven miles from John F. Kennedy International Airport.

They asked if I wanted to land there.

I said that would suit me just fine.

They gave me a radar landing approach and the controller had me slowly losing altitude as I flew closer. The controller asked if I saw the airport. I said no. He said we were close and that he would turn on the high-tension runway lights. Soon I had the runway in sight and was cleared to land.

As we touched down, we saw airliners waiting for us to clear so they could take off. The airport was so large, a vehicle with a red light was sent out to lead us to the parking area.

For readers wondering how, with my hearing disability, I was able to understand radio messages on my approach to JFK, here's the answer: The frequency of the plane's radio was the same as the one frequency I can hear clearly. It is hard for me to understand sounds that are not on that frequency. I never had trouble understanding communications via the radio on the Comanche.

This unscheduled landing coincided with the New York World's Fair. We arranged lodging and went to the fair.

The following morning, the weather was clear to Cape Cod, so we continued our trip, spent a couple of days there with friends, and then flew home.

### Landing gear glitch—and leaking gas

One day Alan and I flew to Asheville, North Carolina, on a business trip. The mountains were covered with clouds as we approached, but the airport was southeast of the city and reporting clear conditions. We were cleared to land and I was in the final approach when I discovered a problem: The plane's landing gear had failed to extend.

I aborted the landing, telling the tower that I was going to fly out of the airport's traffic pattern to see if I could solve the problem. Sure enough, upon checking, I found that the circuit breakers for the landing gear had kicked out. I pushed them back in and the landing gear extended.

That was the first and only time I had trouble with the landing gear.

On a trip to Atlanta with three friends to see a baseball game, I landed at Fulton County airport and parked. I asked the attendant to top off the plane's gas tanks—a pair of 35-gallon inboard wing tanks and two 10-gallon outboard wing tanks—while we were at the game.

After the game, I paid for the gas but did not check the gas caps to be sure they were secure. I should have.

We took off and about fifteen minutes later one of my passengers asked if that was gasoline he saw coming out of one of the outboard wing tanks. It was. The cap was loose, allowing a small stream of gas to escape.

I told everyone I was using gas from that tank, which would lower the amount of gas left. A few minutes later, without warning, the engine started sputtering and the plane slowed. I pushed the nose down to prevent stalling and reached to switch to another gas tank. The engine immediately came back to life.

During the brief interlude, I sensed that my companions were drawing long, uneasy breaths. With everything back to normal, I turned to them. "I don't know about you," I said, "but when something like that happens, I get constipated."

We had a good laugh and continued a safe journey home.

For years, my friends reminded me of my constipation quip.

Where are you?

Three friends and I set out for Daytona Beach, Florida, one February for NASCAR's Daytona 500 stock car race. The weather along the coast was terrible all the way to Florida.

When we landed in Jacksonville, Florida, it was raining at Daytona. Planes were circling the Daytona airport waiting to land. I was told to follow the coastline until I was over Saint Augustine, and then contact Daytona. I did that and we had to circle for about 20 minutes before Daytona called and gave instructions for landing.

The directions were explicit: Fly down the coast to the city, turn right, fly directly to the airport and call when I was ready to land. I followed the instructions, called and they cleared me for landing.

The rain was heavy as I approached the runway. I had landed and was taxiing along when I heard them calling and asking where we were. I replied that I was on the runway directly in front of the control tower.

"You did not come in on the runway we were expecting you to," they said.

"I came in on the first one I saw," I replied.

The morning after the race there was still so much water on the plane I found towels to wipe off the wings because I was afraid to take off a loaded plane with so much water on them.

### Night flight

Once, Maxine and I flew to Orlando, Florida, to visit friends over Easter weekend. On the way home on Easter Monday, we stopped in Warm Springs, Georgia, to visit Franklin D. Roosevelt's Little White House.

The nearest airport was several miles away so we rented a car and drove to the historic site. We had not accounted for the long drive to and from the airport, so by the time we returned there was not enough daylight remaining to make it home by dark.

By my calculations, darkness would fall when we were somewhere over South Carolina. I had flown short distances at night, but Maxine had never been with me. I had always been alone.

I told her that if she wanted to we would stop at an airport before dark, rent a room and spend the night. She said whatever I wanted to do was okay. So, when darkness came halfway across the Palmetto State, we flew on. It was a beautiful night to fly.

I set the plane radio on the radio beacon for Greensboro. When I arrived over the beacon, which was on a hill east of the airport, I asked them to direct me to Asheboro's airport. They gave me directions and we arrived minutes later.

I parked the Comanche, gathered our luggage and we walked to the public telephone at the airport to call our son Richard. He came and picked us up and took us home.

It was a wonderful trip together. I will never forget it.

End of an era

I enjoyed flying the Comanche, but the cost of liability insurance and growing business responsibilities led to the decision to sell the plane.

In 1977, I bought a new Cessna 152. It was a small plane, ideal for renting for training students to fly. I leased the plane to the Asheboro airport, which relieved me of all liability.

I sold that plane when I was seventy and gave up flying forever. I closed Pugh Field and converted the landing strip into a cow pasture and the hangars into sheds for storing farm machinery and hay to feed the cattle.

Being a pilot, owning an airplane, and having a private airstrip had been dreams I lived to see come true. For this, I am thankful.

*A lot of people never accomplish anything for one reason, and one reason only: They're afraid of failure.*

# A New Venture

In 1963, I created a company called General Technicians, dedicated to the sales, installation and servicing of heating and air-conditioning equipment for homes and businesses.

A subsidiary of Pugh Oil Company, the new venture assumed maintenance services formerly handled by Pugh's service department. I served as the manager.

We had our own office building with space for a receptionist, who doubled as a salesperson, a product showroom, and my private office. We had a separate building for the drafting, design and sales departments and one that housed a sheet metal shop and warehouse.

When we began, we sold and installed the systems, subbing electrical, plumbing and other ancillary work to outside technicians. Over time, I realized that depending on others to help complete jobs was costing us time and money, so I added plumbing and electrical services to our repertoire. The addition of appliance sales opened the door for us to deal with new homebuilders.

The company quickly grew beyond my expectations, so I decided to expand. I purchased a lot in Siler City in neighboring Chatham County and hired a contractor to build large brick building with a full basement. The new site offered room for offices and a showroom on the first floor and ample warehouse space below.

The growth continued and we expanded to cover an ever-wider territory. Since we were buying so much equipment and supplies, we received substantial discounts.

Our inventory, accounts receivable, payroll and operating expenses all grew. We were doing a large volume of business, enough to make a profit, but we were not yet doing so.

The answer was not more growth—we were spread out over a large area of installations—but better productivity.

One drawback was that skilled workers were spending too much nonproductive time on the road getting to and from jobsites. Another problem was that those skilled workers too often loaded up their tools and equipment and traveled to a jobsite only to find that the builder was not ready as expected. This typically resulted in the loss of productivity for two of my workers for an entire day.

I was in the prime years of my life, enjoying managing the company and its challenges. I spent hours poring over records, seeking solutions to the problems we faced. In the end, I decided that there were no answers that would result in the company turning a profit. After ten years, I decided to close General Technicians and dedicate all of my energies to the oil company.

I informed employees of my plans to liquidate the company at a meeting and explained that the shutdown would be gradual. Some would stay on the payroll longer than others as we took inventory and completed all installations under contract.

A few months later, we had completed all of the work and had sold all of the company's assets, including a large inventory of equipment and supplies. I paid all the company's outstanding accounts, including bank loans and taxes, and forever closed the doors on General Technicians.

Was the business a failure?

I don't think so.

For ten years, the company employed a number of people and paid a large amount of money for salaries.

For ten years, the company bought and sold a large amount of equipment manufactured by many people, thus creating jobs.

For ten years, the company sold and installed a large amount of heating and air-conditioning equipment in homes and businesses and paid a large amount in local, state and federal taxes.

And for ten years, General Technicians was a respected member of the business community.

A failure? No.

I would classify the liquidation of the company as an orderly retreat from the business world with dignity and integrity.

*You know, life can be fun. I've enjoyed living.*

# North to Alaska

I JOINED A group of North Carolina oil jobbers on a ten-day tour of Alaska in 1974. The itinerary included visits to the North Slope oil fields at Prudhoe Bay, to the deepwater port of Valdez, which would serve as the terminal of the Alaskan oil pipeline from the oil fields, and to see the ongoing construction of the pipeline that would carry crude oil 800 miles from the oil fields to Valdez.

We switched planes several times as we journeyed from the East Coast to the forty-ninth state. We boarded an airliner in North Carolina bound for Seattle, Washington, and then took a jumbo jet bound for Japan. We got off at the first stop, Anchorage, Alaska, and caught a smaller plane for a 450-mile flight to Fairbanks, where we spent the night. The next morning we headed to Point Barrow and then flew the final leg to Prudhoe Bay.

I was amazed at what had been accomplished in establishing an oil-producing field in this remote part of the planet.

The ocean which ships had to sail to deliver heavy equipment needed for the massive project was frozen most of the year. The window of ice-free weather was just a few months.

Construction included buildings to house the workers and all of the accessory operations, as well as installation of equipment to supply the water, heat and electricity necessary for such a gigantic undertaking.

The employee facilities were comfortable and well furnished. We ate a meal in the dining room and it was good. Workers flown in from Anchorage clocked several days before rotating out for a new crew. The harsh conditions also necessitated special care for equipment: Parked vehicles were kept plugged into a heating device to keep the engine warm so they would start in the extreme cold.

On a tour of the oil fields we saw wells pumping crude oil and huge stockpiles of pipe. Without seeing it in person, it would be hard to imagine the size of the pipe—and the amount—needed for the 800-mile-long project.

The landing strip where we boarded a plane for the return trip to Fairbanks was not paved. I heard gravel flying up behind us as we took off. The flight took us over the Arctic mountain range, a vast, rugged wilderness. It is not a place one would want to be alone.

We took a train from Fairbanks to Anchorage the following morning and I pondered what I had seen: The awesome accomplishments of man in dealing with the awesome forces of nature.

There were few stops along the 450-mile ride to Anchorage. We passed few towns, just a small village every once in a while. Mostly we traveled across wide-open space, miles and miles of barren, wide-open space.

Sometimes, we encountered someone, or several someones, standing by the lonely tracks waiting for the train. We stopped and picked them up. Where they came from, how far they were going, and why, I have no idea.

It reminded me of a time, way back in 1918, when my mother and I got onto a train at four o'clock in the morning in the little mill village of Franklinville. We were headed to the big city of Greensboro, about forty miles away as the crow flies.

The engine pulled a passenger car, a car for baggage and mail, and several box cars. The track wound through a number of villages along the way. We stopped at each one to pick up passengers and mail or to switch loaded freight cars. We also came upon people standing by the tracks waiting for the train, and we stopped and picked them up.

Nine hours later, we reached Greensboro.

I am not comparing the railroad in Alaska in 1974 with the railroad in my home state of North Carolina in 1918. I am simply pointing out that there were some similarities with the train trip I took when I was five.

The train to Anchorage passed near the majestic Mount McKinley. The train stopped at a station so passengers could get off for sightseeing and the view of the snow- and ice-covered peak was awe-inspiring.

Another sight that made a lasting impression on me was a gigantic stuffed polar bear, standing upright on its hind legs, in the lobby of an Anchorage hotel. A sign said the bear was sixteen feet tall.

Alaska is a land of many lakes. Every town we visited was near a body of water. I do not recall seeing many automobiles, but I saw a lot of small planes. In each town we saw airplanes outfitted with pontoons or floats for landing on water; we also saw planes that could land on water or land.

From Anchorage, we rode 450 miles by bus to Valdez. We stopped at a roadside diner for lunch. The wooden building rested on a group of crossed up logs. The construction prevented the heat from the building from transferring to the frozen ground, which would lead to thawing and affect the stability of the structure.

The highway followed alongside an inland glacier for many miles. The glacier was slowly making its way to the sea, leaving behind a bed of gravel and rock.

We toured the site where the oil terminal was being built in Valdez, a town flanked by mountains on one side and a beautiful natural harbor on the other. The harbor is ice-free year round. Ships sail from Valdez through the Prince William Sound to the Pacific Ocean.

We boarded a ship in Valdez that carried us through the Gulf of Alaska to Seward. It was a scenic trip, sometimes with mountains on either side of the boat. We passed numerous fishing boats and detoured around some so we would not disturb their fishing. We also visited a huge glacier that was depositing large pieces of ice into the water.

Seward was accessible only by ship, airplane, or train. Our bus in Seward was driven onto a railroad flatcar that took us to the highway leading to Anchorage. We flew from Anchorage to Seattle the next morning, ending an eventful ten days.

We had seen a widely varied landscape by plane, ship, bus and railroad, from the frozen Arctic oil fields to the warm waters of Valdez. Alaska covers a huge swath of our earth and has a little of almost everything nature has to offer.

On farming: *It probably extended my life longer. My wife didn't like it. She wanted me to come home and sit down in the rocking chair. I feel that somehow or another I'm expected to do more than just that.*

## Back to the Land

IN 1983, I made a life-changing decision: I sold my business interests in Pugh Oil Company to my oldest son, Richard, and embarked on a new career as a farmer.

I was seventy and felt as if I had accomplished most of the things that I viewed as my personal responsibilities. I had paid for good educations for each of my sons and had helped each of them get started in their chosen professions.

During my years as a businessman, I had received a lot of assistance from friends, neighbors, customers, suppliers and business associates. To all of them, I extend sincere appreciation.

In turn, I had frequently been able to help others. It was a privilege and pleasure to be part of my community.

My wife and I had been married for forty-nine years, through which we shared our ups and downs. We had traveled together on business and for pleasure in our car, in our airplane and on public airplanes.

She had worked all of our married lives, but was now retired and enjoying time with our children, grandchildren, and great-grandchildren.

I grew up on a farm and have always had a love for the land and the world of nature. I never had any desire to become a man of wealth and power, so when I left the daily duties of running an oil company behind I turned back to the land and nature.

Over the years, whenever they became available, I had acquired small tracts that adjoined my home property. By 1983, this amounted to two hundred acres made up mostly of cutover timberland.

It was a rugged landscape of hills and hollows crisscrossed by streams and dotted with rocks and tree stumps. I sold my airplane, bought a bulldozer and started clearing the land.

I planned to create a breeding farm for registered cattle.

You could say my early days on the bulldozer amounted to on-the-job training. Like many other things I had tackled in my life, climbing onto the powerful machine intent on clearing land was a learning process.

I persevered through early problems by following my personal motto: Just plain old staying with it.

I steadily improved and eventually got pretty good at it.

The days were long. I started at daybreak, worked until noon, took a forty-five-minute break, then climbed back onto the dozer and worked until the sun went down.

The bulldozer never got tired, but I sure did. Even though the work was hard, I enjoyed it, and I've found that if you're doing something you enjoy, you do not feel tired until the day is done.

I filled hollows by pushing stumps, loose rock and other debris into the low places. When a spot was filled, I covered everything with about two feet of dirt to create a seedbed in which to sow seed to grow hay to harvest or grass for cattle to graze. I spread fertilizer using a farm tractor but sowed the seed using a hand-cranked spreader strapped around my shoulders. After clearing each section and sowing seed, I built a fence around it.

The availability of water and shade dictated the size of each pasture. When completed, the once rugged landscape was going to be beautiful: two hundred acres of green pastures among rolling hills, small valleys, stands of trees and spring-fed streams.

Overlooking all of this was the tallest hill on my property. From the top, you could see in all directions.

*I've got two afflictions. I'm hard of hearing. The other one is I'm hardheaded. I guess that probably the best trait I was born with was determination.*

# Here Come the Cows

It took a year to get ready to add cows: to clear enough land, to prepare enough pasture and to have a cattle barn built.

I purchased my first registered breeding cows from an established breeder in Dayton, Ohio. I left North Carolina to fly to Ohio on a cold January day. It was 45 degrees and raining. When I arrived at the farm in Dayton, it was five below zero with snow on the ground.

The farm owner and I rode around his farm, comfortable in an enclosed cab on a John Deere tractor, so I could survey his cattle. The ground was frozen hard as cement. I selected ten young cows and made arrangements for them to be delivered to my farm.

The next step was breeding. I ordered semen from well-known cattle breeders from around the country who had outstanding registered bulls, assuring that calves from my cows would be above average.

Since I had to wait nine months to have calves to sell, I got back to the job of clearing land for pasture. As each year passed, I opened more and more sections of pastureland.

I expanded my herd by adding cows I had artificially bred and by buying young cows from other breeders. I entered bull calves I had bred in "test stations" established by the state in various locations. These bulls ate special feed for several weeks before being evaluated for weight gain and breeding ability. Then they were sold at auction.

Every year my bulls entered in the station rated in the top 10 percent in performance. Some years, I was fortunate enough to have the top performing bull, which always brought the highest price at the sale.

The more involved I was with my herd, the less time I had for creating pasture – and I still had a lot of clearing to do.

After ten years of working on the farm by myself, when I was eighty, I hired some help. Kelly Wicker, who was in his early twenties, was a hard worker, a quick learner, and very good at whatever he did.

I bought a track front-end loader for clearing land and operated it; Kelly manned the bulldozer. We tended to the cattle and then we climbed aboard our machines and cleared land.

Along the way, I traveled to auction sales of cattle at breeding farms in North Carolina and Virginia. Besides learning what other breeders were doing to improve their herds, I learned how to buy cattle at auction. Sometimes I brought cattle home and resold them at a profit. I also continued attending the test stations.

While I was away, Kelly took care of the farm. Everything on the farm was going well. We continued to clear land for pasture and growing hay. I was selling herd bulls and cows to other breeders around the country. And we harvested enough hay every summer to feed my herd in the winter and to sell to other farmers.

Having good equipment was a key. In addition to the track loader and bulldozer, I had three farm tractors. Two of them had front-end loaders that were useful in a variety of ways, including moving hay and spreading fertilizer.

My farm was a model operation of efficiency.

It was a pleasure to manage.

*I've done a lot of things I never dreamed of doing.*
*I've done a lot of things I was told I couldn't do.*
*The sum total of me – I'm thankful for what I have,*
*for the friends and the opportunities to do the things I have.*

# A Boyhood Dream Come True

WHEN I WAS working in the hosiery mill, I had time to read a lot of books. I was always interested in the natural world, and in stories of adventurers in the wild.

I read about early explorers of the Grand Canyon and the Colorado River—and how they tried to navigate, in wooden boats, the mighty, untamed river that stretched nearly 1,500 miles from the Rocky Mountains to the Pacific Ocean. Several lost their lives in the attempt.

In 1994, at the age of eighty-one, I did something I had long dreamed of doing: rafting the Colorado. I left Kelly in charge of the farm and flew with two friends to Las Vegas, Nevada, where we caught a bus for a five hundred-mile ride to Arizona.

There we set out in rubber boats on an adventure—eight days and seven nights on the Colorado River. We spent days in the boats, making frequent stops to hike up side canyons along the river. At night, we slept on mats by the river's edge.

Our party, led by guides, traveled in two boats, twelve to a boat.

Rapids are common along the Colorado. Some are larger, higher and more dangerous to navigate and they constantly change due to storms.

When we set out the water was clear. One night a thunderstorm struck upriver. Upon awakening, we found a raging red muddy torrent sweeping large rocks downstream. Our guides beached the boats when we came to rapids and walked along the riverbank to determine if the storm had deposited new boulders.

A guide must determine where the main current is going over the rapids and must keep the boat in this current to clear the rocks at the top. At the bottom of the rapids, a solid sheet of water shoots over the boat. Those in the front hold onto ropes to keep from being knocked out of the boat by the water's force.

I enjoyed running the rapids.

Each day we encountered different scenes and different kinds of rock formations. We also saw places where some of the long-ago explorers lost their lives, and even the wooden remains of some of their boats.

Along some stretches, the water was swift and smooth and we could look up and see the rim of the canyon thousands of feet overhead. In some places, the river ran straight ahead as far as we could see before disappearing around a bend.

Around one of those bends, we came upon a large cave carved out by the current over time. We got out to explore. The cave floor, covered with sand, was higher than the normal flow of the river.

Our guide told us that Indians had used the cave as a meeting place and that it could hold about 30,000 people. Some of us played a game using plastic bats and balls in the cave. It was a fantastic experience.

Today, the Colorado River has large dams and lakes that generate electric power for millions. It provides water for hundreds of cities and to irrigate thousands of acres of land.

The river is fairly tame compared to what the Indians or the early explorers saw. But there are places where a visitor can get a glimpse, and a feeling, of what it used to be.

One is awed by the canyon and the river and what they provide for millions of people, and by what man has done to make this happen.

On the eighth day of our trip, we reach the mouth of the canyon on Lake Mead. From there speedboats zipped us across the lake to buses waiting to take us back to the modern world.

As a boy working in the hosiery mill, I had read about the mighty river with awe and wished that I could see it for myself, never really considering that it might one day happen.

The trip was a dream come true.

I am thankful I had the opportunity.

*You learn a lot by looking. Observing.*

# Another Northern Excursion

AN OPPORTUNITY TO travel somewhere else I wanted to go came about when I was eighty-four. I read an article in a cattle magazine about an upcoming seminar in Canada on growing forage for cattle herds.

I had hoped one day to visit the city of Vancouver in the province of British Columbia, where the three-day seminar would be held. This was a chance to combine sightseeing with a business trip to learn from well-known professors of agronomy at leading Western agricultural universities.

My wife agreed to go with me. We flew to Seattle, Washington, rented a car and drove the remaining two hundred miles to Vancouver so I could see the countryside.

We attended seminar meetings in the evenings and at night; by day, we toured the city, including a sightseeing trip by boat in a beautiful harbor, where ships bound for Alaska depart. On the third day, we took a bus trip along the Fraser River to a Canadian government agricultural test station, where we enjoyed a barbecue meal on the grounds.

We sat opposite a professor of agronomy from the University of Ames in Iowa and his wife, who confided that they had a problem. The professor was going to be honored that night for his achievements, and he had not packed any ties.

I told them I had several neckties and would be happy to loan him one. When we returned to the hotel, they came to our room and picked out a tie. After the seminar, they came back to our room to return the tie and thank me. To this day, I do not know what his name was.

I have kept in touch, however, with Dr. Tom Pittman, another person I met at the seminar. At the time, he was a young veterinarian working for the government in the province. Since we met, he moved to work as top veterinarian for a large cattle company operating feedlots in the stockyards of Calgary.

A few years ago he applied for a teaching position with the University of Calgary. He has graduated his first four-year class and is teaching his second four-year group. I spent three days visiting Tom, his wife and their two sons in 2010.

I am proud of his accomplishments and thankful for his friendship.

We drove back to Seattle with eight days left on our planned ten-day trip and set out to tour the states of Washington and Oregon. I especially wanted to visit Mount Ranier, Mount Adams, Mount St. Helen's and Mount Hood.

Mount Ranier is a massive accumulation of rocks, snow and ice; Mount Adams, a smaller snow-covered mountain, is shaped like a volcano; truly a beautiful sight, Mt. St. Helen's is a massive, volcanic peak that exploded a few years ago and destroyed all the trees for miles around—an awesome scene of destruction testifying to the power and relentless fury of nature.

We drove across Washington to the town of Ellenburgh, near Spokane, where we spent the day with friends. From there we followed the course of the mighty Columbia River to Oregon. At Portland, Oregon, we crossed the river and followed it to the Pacific Ocean.

We drove along the coast, which is rugged compared to the Atlantic coast of North Carolina, to central Oregon. I wanted to visit the state's seed-growing region; all of the seed sown on my farm came from this place. I was fascinated to tour the seed farms and learn about the process of growing, harvesting and preparing seed for shipment.

When we visited Mount Hood I remembered the picture of the beautiful mountain on crates of Oregon-grown apples in stores when I was a boy.

*I never wanted to be stuck in anything long.*

# Out of a Job

KELLY HAD BEEN working for me for five years in 1998 when he decided to leave my farm and start his own business. He was twenty-five and I encouraged him to set out and begin building his own future.

On the other hand, I was eighty-five.

I had accomplished what I had set out to do fifteen years earlier. I had created a successful cattle-breeding farm with one hundred registered cows, ninety-four registered calves, and three registered bulls on two hundred acres of pastureland. I owned all the equipment needed to maintain the operation.

I had had a dream and I had lived my dream. For that I was thankful. But no one in my family had an interest in taking over the business if anything happened to me.

Registered cattle are more valuable as breeding animals than those raised for beef, so I decided to sell my breeding animals.

There were two ways to do this: Hold an auction or find buyers.

If I had an auction, I would have to hire an auctioneer, advertise the sale and then cross my fingers. I had been to enough auctions to know that the seller has to take whatever the high bidder is willing to pay. Then he has to pay the auctioneer.

In all the sales I had attended the sum total for all the cattle sold was less than they were worth. I decided to sell the cattle myself.

I went to see a man who had been in the cattle business all his life, a man I could trust. I told him I had priced each head of cattle I had and asked what he would want in compensation to help me sell them. He said 10 percent. It was a fair amount.

In six months, the two of us found buyers for all of my cattle at my price less the 10 percent I paid my friend for helping. I sold all of my equipment except for one tractor and a mowing machine and leased the farm to another cattle breeder.

For the first time since I was fifteen, I did not have a job or a business to run.

But in seventy years in the world of work, I had learned a lot about people and what does (and does not) work in everyday life. Most of all, I had learned a lot about myself.

I also had learned the value of knowledge and experience and that sometimes you can create your own opportunities.

I am thankful for all the good things that happened to me.

It is best to forget the bad.

I did not have any idea what was in store for me. But life on earth is worth living and making the best from what it gives you. And that is what I planned to do with the rest of whatever time I had left.

*I've never been a pessimist, but I have been a realist.*

# Home Sweet Home

AN EVENT OCCURRED in February 1996 that could have been a disaster.

I was sitting in the den reading the newspaper and my wife, Maxine, was in the kitchen cooking. She screamed.

I jumped up and rushed to the kitchen. The oven door was standing open and flames and black smoke were rolling out. Something she had been baking had exploded out of the oven onto the floor and it was on fire.

Right away I realized it was a grease fire, which generates a lot of black smoke and soot. I slammed the oven door shut, ran into the den and pulled a heavy throw rug off the floor. I threw it onto the fire on the kitchen floor to smother the flames and turned off all the switches on the stove. Closing the oven door had cut off the oxygen supply and smothered that fire too.

Maxine had run out of the house through the dining room. When the fire was out I followed, rushing into the fresh air covered in soot and suffering from smoke inhalation.

I was eighty-two.

One of my neighbors later asked me why I had not called the fire department. I replied that there had not been time. If we had waited for the fire department to arrive to put out the fire, it would have been too late.

We would have had to watch the house we had built in 1949—seven rooms, two bathrooms, a laundry room, a two-car-garage and all our possessions—go up in flames.

Smoke and soot had spread throughout the house. It was a real mess. Virtually everything had to be cleaned: walls, ceilings, floors, curtains, bed linens, dishes, pots and pans. Clothes in the closets had to be laundered or dry cleaned.

After they were cleaned, the walls and ceilings had to be repainted. We needed new tile in the kitchen. We had to buy a new stove.

A friend who had a business nearby handled all the work. We knew we could trust them; it is a privilege and pleasure to have business people like John Woodell in your community.

It took several weeks, but when they were finished, the house where we had lived for forty-seven years was like new inside.

We enjoyed living in the house together until Maxine passed away in 2007. I lived alone in the house until January 2012 when health problems necessitated that I move to a new home, Clapp's Mountain Top Living in Asheboro.

*Man's life is spirit, mind and body. The spirit dictates to the brain and the brain dictates to the body. What a man really needs is this: He needs a healthy spirit. He needs a healthy mind; this is subject to the spirit. And he needs a healthy body, the vessel.*

# Lessons in Healthy Living

IN MY FIRST eight decades on earth, I experienced no serious illnesses and always thought of myself as a healthy individual.

The landscape changed when a doctor told me I had an enlarged prostate, which can lead to prostate cancer. Not long after that, an eye doctor gave me more disquieting news: I had progressive macular degeneration in one eye. I was eighty.

A year later, I had an attack of diverticulitis—the first of many—that landed me in the hospital so they could stop the bleeding and give me a transfusion. I wound up needing two pints of blood.

The realization hit me that I really had very little knowledge of what healthy living was all about. I set out to change that. Throughout my life I had relied on books to learn how to do things, from building a house to flying a plane.

Now I turned my attention to healthy living, determined to explore good nutrition, exercise, vitamins, herbs and the effects of medicine on one's body.

My doctors had told me there was no cure for diverticulitis or for macular degeneration. I began to order and read books on food, nutrition, vitamins, herbs and supplements. I took out subscriptions to several health magazines and was intrigued by articles about real people and their search for answers to their own health problems.

I was not interested in standard remedies that could be found in medical texts. I was inclined to think that I could learn more from the personal experiences of people facing ailments, and I think that proved to be the right idea.

Within a few months, I had gathered enough information from various sources to locate two supplements to get me started in the treatment of my enlarged prostate and my macular degeneration. I also changed my diet to include foods recommended for the prostate and the eyes.

I have been on the diet and the supplements for nineteen years.

My prostate has gotten smaller. It has not given me any trouble.

And it seems that the macular degeneration in my right eye stopped progressing. When I turned ninety-five, my driver's license was up for renewal. I passed the written and driving tests for a five-year renewal. The only restriction is that I wear my eyeglasses when I drive.

The diverticulitus was a different story. Over eighteen years, I had ten attacks. With a single exception, I was hospitalized and had a blood transfusion every time. I spent three days in the hospital after the last attack, too, but the loss of blood was minimal and the bleeding stopped without treatment.

I have no idea why the last attack was so "mild," but the way I see it, my regimen may not be a cure for diverticulitis, but perhaps it has protected my colon from further damage. And maybe from cancer.

Since 1998, I have stuck to a high-fiber diet of fruits, berries, vegetables, certain kinds of fish, and very little red meat, coupled with daily doses of certain vitamins, herbs, and other supplements.

*The bare-knuckled truth: Taking it easy never accomplished anything. Nothing complicated about that.*

# Move It, Move It, Move It

WHEN I WAS eighty-seven, I joined the local YMCA and embarked on a regular routine of exercise. I was the oldest member.

Dr. Glenn Dawson asked me to join his class of seniors at the Y who participated in the yearly senior games. I told him I was too busy. He asked again the next year and I decided to join. It was a decision I have never regretted.

Why would I?

Since my first foray into the world of competition with other senior adults, I have participated in local, state and national games. Over the past dozen years, I have met a lot of people, and made a lot of friends from my area, from around the state, and from across the nation.

An added bonus: I have been fortunate enough to win some medals. I've collected quite a lot of them actually.

The National Senior Games are staged every two years. My first experience at that grand event came in Norfolk, Virginia, in 2003.

I had learned to play racquetball at the Asheboro Y when I was eighty-nine. Being the oldest racquetball participant at both the local and state games, I earned an automatic gold medal (after proving that I could play the game by taking to the court against a younger player).

In Norfolk, I had competition in my age bracket. We played. He won. But I had earned my first national games medal, a silver one.

I qualified for and entered three events at the national games in Pittsburgh, Pennsylvania, in 2005, adding shot put and discus to racquetball. I rode to Pittsburgh with Dr. Dawson and two others, a mother and daughter. About halfway to Pennsylvania, we made a rest stop.

I went to the restroom and had a bowel movement. Red blood in the stool was a red flag—it was an attack of diverticulitis.

I should have heeded the warning and headed home, but I didn't. I hoped that the bleeding would stop. And I didn't say a word to the others.

When we got to Pittsburgh I bought several cans of baby food, telling my traveling companions that it was my remedy for an upset stomach. The soft food did help lessen the amount of blood I was losing, but did not stop it.

I competed in the shot put and discus competitions and earned a bronze medal in each. The others in my group finished their events on a Friday and left for home. My last event was set for Monday afternoon.

That morning, I packed my bags and left them in the hotel checkout room. I went to the gym at Pittsburgh University, where my racquetball match was scheduled for 1:00 p.m. At noon, I headed to the courts. My opponent never showed up.

By default, I was the gold medal winner.

But, as the rules state, I had to prove that I could play.

The officials found an opponent (remember, I did not have to beat him, I simply had to show that I could play racquetball). I recall meeting him and talking before going onto the court.

The next thing I remember is waking up four days later in the Pittsburgh University Hospital with Richard, my oldest son, by my side. While we were playing, I had collapsed on the court. I was rushed to the hospital and given a blood transfusion. The doctors said I had suffered heart failure.

I was released to fly home where I was to check in at Randolph Hospital in Asheboro. A friend from home, Dr. James Rich, was attending the games. He offered to fly Richard and me home in his private plane. We accepted the generous offer.

Back home in the hospital, I was being treated for internal bleeding and heart conditions. My digestive doctor treated me for eight days before he was able to get the bleeding to stop.

I got to go home for two weeks to recuperate, then entered a High Point hospital where my heart doctor was going to perform a heart catheterization. During the procedure he discovered a blocked artery and installed a stent.

The physician also prescribed four medications. I asked him how long I would have to take the medicines. The rest of your life, he replied. I don't think so, I said.

I was ninety-one. I did not think I had a heart problem.

I was pretty sure that my heart failure had been caused by the loss of blood. Nothing else. And I knew that the prescribed medications had side effects which could affect other vital organs if taken for a long period of time.

When I got out of the hospital, I did a stress test at my heart doctor's office. He hooked me to a monitor and showed me pictures of my heart at work. Nothing I saw proved to me that I had a problem with my heart.

So, when I had finished taking the original prescriptions, I did not have them refilled. It's been nine years and I still do not have any heart problems that I know of.

*No man who's ever lived in the history of mankind knows what's next. It's awesome. But I think there is something next. If you've followed the rules as laid down by our Creator. You've got to have faith.*

## My Beloved

IN 2001, WHEN my wife, Maxine, was eighty-three, she started having health problems and started seeing a doctor in Greensboro every month. We made the trip to see him every month for six years.

She was taking several prescription medications, but her condition gradually got worse.

We had been married for seventy-three years when she died on May 6, 2007. She was eighty-nine.

I loved my wife and I miss her very much, but I watched her suffer for so long with no cure in sight. I knew that her suffering had come to an end. I believe that when anyone becomes terminally ill, death is a blessing.

Maxine left me many wonderful memories and a large family of loving, caring children, grandchildren, great-grandchildren and, yes, even great-great-grandchildren. When I am with our children, Maxine is present in spirit.

I can also add the many friends we enjoyed during our long lives together here on earth.

Prior to her death, Maxine made her own final arrangements with the funeral home. She wanted a simple graveside service and that is what we gave her.

Everyone gathered for food and fellowship in the church fellowship hall after the service. After joining family and friends for a short while, I left and went home to the farm.

A brief thunderstorm passed through the area not long after the service. That evening I got in my car and drove the few miles to the cemetery. I parked my car near Maxine's grave, got out and stood there for several minutes, looking down.

Memories flooded my mind as the setting sun shined on my face. For some reason, I turned and looked to the east, where I saw a rainbow. I stood, my eyes filled with tears, drinking in the dazzling beauty, when I realized something: The rainbow was a personal message to let me know that Maxine was with the angels in heaven.

*It's amazing I've been able to do these things at my age, but I've been used to getting the job done all my life, one way or another.*

# O Canada!

I HAD READ a great deal about the Canadian Rockies and their great national parks and dreamed of visiting the place.

In June 2009, I decided to make the dream a reality. I planned a ten-day excursion—eight days hiking and sightseeing in the Rockies and two days visiting an old friend.

I took a plane from Greensboro to Toronto, then a longer airplane ride to Calgary in western Canada. From there, a bus delivered me to the Canadian Rockies.

My first stop was Lake Louise, one of the most beautiful places I have ever seen. I lodged at the Chateau Lake Louise, a luxury hotel built by the railroad companies to accommodate wealthy tourists who traveled by train to the Rockies.

The magnificent hotel overlooks the lake, which is surrounded by magnificent mountains covered in ice and snow.

My first night there, I gazed out at a spectacular landscape while dining in the hotel dining room. I mentally compared the panoramic vista to pictures I had viewed years earlier, back home in North Carolina.

I realized I was living a dream.

For a moment, I felt a little like Cinderella.

The next day, the tour bus took me to Banff, the largest town in a park by the same name. The park, sprinkled with lovely mountain lakes, is home to an assortment of game animals.

The area also boasts an array of attractions for visitors to enjoy year-round. One of my favorites was a ride in a gondola traveling over a steel cable stretched between two mountains. The trip covers 5,120 feet at 13 feet per second to an elevation of 7,486 feet.

I probably do not have to say it, but I will.

Hanging suspended in a small metal bucket attached to a cable more than a mile above the valley floor—a contraption with four seats but no wings, no propeller, and no landing gear—is simply breathtaking.

Next door to Branff is Jasper National Park, which encompasses the Columbia ice fields and the Athabasca glacier, whose melting ice forms the headwaters of several rivers. Some of the waters run deep underground; you can hear it, but you cannot see it.

I spent a night in the railroad town of Jasper. I was surprised to see so much railroad traffic in the Rockies, even though the trains mostly carry freight, not passengers.

Most of my tour companions were from Asia, including travelers from India, and some from Europe. I became friends with a couple from Scotland in the British Isles. We took many meals together and did a little sightseeing together. Once, we saw mountain goats grazing alongside the road; another time, we passed a large bull elk by the shoulder of the road.

The most amazing experience of the trip was boarding a special vehicle in Jasper National Park for a ride into the mountains on the glacier.

Above the timberline we came upon huge piles of gravel. It looked as if someone on a bulldozer had been hard at work. But what we were seeing was the work of nature.

Snow falling on the mountain of rock freezes into ice, which slides slowly down the rock surface, gradually grinding the surface down. I believe that in time, nature will grind the rock down to the timberline and trees will grow on the top of the Canadian Rockies.

The forces of nature are constantly at work, changing our world. Man has changed much in our world, but it is my belief that we will never be able to conquer the forces of nature.

My next stop was at the home of my friend Dr. Tom Pittman, who lives in Calgary in the province of Alberta. I stayed with him and his family for two days. He and I had been friends for a dozen years, but it was only the second time we had met in person.

Calgary has the largest number of cattle feedlots in all of Canada. Dr. Pittman, formerly the head veterinarian for a large feedlot company, was now teaching veterinary science at the University of Calgary. With my background operating a registered cattle-breeding farm, he and I had common interests.

During my visit, we drove to the Calgary feedlots. It was the most cattle I had ever seen in a single location. One feedlot had 50,000 cattle, each topping the scales at 1,200 pounds.

We toured the state-of-the-art veterinary science building where he worked and I met the faculty. The leading member of the faculty was a breeder of registered Angus cattle, just like I had been for fifteen years. He gave me a picture of himself with one of his prize-winning cows.

Canada is a large nation with vast natural resources and is very conservative regarding its environment.

I have visited three times. The country has much to offer to visitors or someone seeking a career and home. I admired the things I saw in Canada and have enjoyed my experiences north of the border.

We are fortunate to have them as our neighbors.

*I'll be a winner whether I bring home a medal or not. I'm a winner just for participating. I'll meet new friends. I'll come home with a new batch of names in my notebook.*

## The Games Go On

I MISSED THE 2007 National Senior Games due to Maxine's death, but journeyed to San Francisco, California, for the 2009 games.

I traveled alone, flying to the West Coast, to once again compete in three events, racquetball, shot put and discus.

A room in a dormitory at Stanford University, one of the premier universities in the United States, would be home for fifteen days. The facilities were first-class, large and accessible. I could catch a bus and ride for free to and from any place on campus. The bus stopped right in front of the dorm.

There were ten thousand senior athletes representing all fifty states.

We stayed busy and were greeted warmly everywhere we went. If we were not participating in an event, we watched others perform. I spent a lot of time watching basketball competition and events at the track. I also was a spectator for badminton and table tennis games and tennis and volleyball matches.

I met many new friends. One was a volunteer at a basketball game. His name was Michael Hess and he was an assistant for the basketball program.

His home was in Newport Beach, California, where his parents lived. Michael, who was forty-five, had graduated from the University of California at Irving, where he was a star basketball player. He also had played professional basketball in Germany for three years. He had a PhD in sports management and taught at a university in Madrid, Spain, after his pro career.

We were both interested in the senior games association and in promoting exercise and a healthy lifestyle for senior citizens. We exchanged addresses and agreed to keep in touch by phone or by computer. He was very good with computers.

About a year after the 2009 games—from which I brought home gold medals in discus and racquetball and a silver in shot put, by the way—a vacancy opened up on the board of directors for the senior games' national organization. I encouraged Mike to apply.

I thought the board would benefit from a talented and energetic younger person. Those in a position to make the decision agreed. He got the job.

At the 2011 senior games in Houston, he was in charge of the basketball program and did an outstanding job. Then he set his sights on planning and promoting the 2013 games in Cleveland, Ohio, in which I set my sights on competing in the one hundred-year-old category.

*I was born on Columbus Day. He was an adventurer and so was I. The difference was the path we followed.*

# A Forbidding but Beautiful Place

JANUARY 2010 BROUGHT another journey I had long dreamed of taking when I joined a small group of people on a small adventure ship bound for the bottom of the world: Antarctica and the South Pole.

The ship carried just one hundred passengers and there were no elevators on board. Stairs took us up and down between decks.

At ninety-six, I was by far the oldest person making the trip.

I was traveling alone, having flown from Greensboro, North Carolina, to Houston, Texas, and then to Buenos Aires in Argentina, where the large metropolitan airport is extremely busy.

Planes and people come and go from around the world. The terminal and its surroundings are congested with people speaking a variety of languages. Many people are holding signs with their names on them. I was one of them.

The person scheduled to pick me up and take me to a smaller airport for the next leg of the journey was looking for my sign. When we finally connected, he approached and indicated that I should follow him to the car.

He did not speak English. I do not speak Spanish. We drove for an hour without speaking a word. When we arrived at the smaller airport, I got out of the car. He waved good-bye and drove away.

My flight carried me to Ushuaia, Argentina, which officially bills itself as the southernmost city in the world. I spent the night at a hotel in this coastal outpost where I met the man who would be my roommate on the voyage to Antarctica. He was forty-seven, a computer expert from the Netherlands, and a nice fellow. But he never had much to say to me.

Perhaps it was the difference in our ages. Perhaps it was the fact that he was not married and had an eye for the ladies. Whatever it was, he made his friends on the trip and I made mine.

We boarded the ship the next afternoon. I had never been on a large boat before. When we left the harbor, the water was smooth and when I crawled into my bunk to sleep that first night, the water was still calm.

I did not know—and no one had warned me—that we were headed for the Drake Passage, which I now know is known as having some of the roughest ocean waters in the world.

During the night I awakened to find that the ship, and, of course, my bunk, was pitching and rocking. I needed to go to the bathroom so I got up. It was a bad choice. The rolling of the boat sent me ricocheting off the wall of the cabin. I managed to grab the bathroom door as I hurtled past. In the bathroom, I bounced off another wall then grabbed onto the toilet. When I was done, I crawled back to bed on my hands and knees.

I escaped with only bruises, but the next morning, I took note of things to hold onto to navigate around the cabin should a similar situation arise. I made a mental note of them and never ricocheted off a wall again for the duration of the trip.

We sailed into smoother waters and a land unlike any I had ever seen: The land was covered in snow and ice and ice floated in the water; it was cold, very, very cold. We sailed between mountains sheathed in snow and ice, which was slowly sliding into the ocean and breaking off to form icebergs.

I saw no sign of animal life at this point in the journey.

It was deathly quiet. The hum of the ship's engines was the only sound. The landscape was beautiful, an awesome sight, but it was also forbidding, leaving me with a feeling that we did not belong there.

Soon we had passed the mountains into an area of low hills, ridges and rock outcroppings where we saw signs of life: penguins and seals.

Animals in this part of the world depend on warm ocean waters to survive. The penguins find their food in the sea, and the seals eat the penguins, which must be among the toughest creatures alive to survive this harsh environment.

They are lovely animals at a decided disadvantage on land as they can neither fly nor run. In the water, however, they are fast, graceful swimmers.

One day during the trip I was onshore, sitting on a barrel, when a long line of penguins, padding along in single file with about fifteen feet between them, passed by no more than twenty feet away. It was remarkable.

One penguin stopped directly opposite me. He (or she) looked at me. I looked at him (or her). The magnificent black-and-white bird shook its head a couple of times, and then moved on.

I have often wondered what that penguin was thinking. I would like to know. I have also wondered if penguins are truly God's creatures—and I think they are—why are they there in such a harsh and forbidding place and what role do they play in God's creation?

*We were a bunch of adventurers.*
*If you couldn't take care of yourself you were in the wrong place.*

## The Oldest Visitor

EVERY DAY, THE ship set anchor to allow the more adventuresome to go ashore.

To get to shore we had to negotiate a stairway fastened to the side of the ship and then get into a small rubber boat bobbing in the water. It was a tricky maneuver decked out in three layers of clothing, rubber boots and life jackets, but a pair of guides helped keep us from falling into the sea.

The little boats powered by outboard engines seated twelve. The boats were beached in shallow water near the shore and we waded the rest of the way.

There was really little to see save, near the water, penguins and seals, and then inland, for as far as the eye could see, vast empty stretches of ice and snow.

On my third day in Antarctica, I donned swimming trunks under my usual three layers of clothes before heading ashore. Why? Because I planned to participate in what is called "the polar bear plunge."

The ship's doctor didn't want me to do it. The ship's expedition leader didn't want me to do it. They tried to talk me out of it. They were afraid my heart would stop. I really didn't think much about it. I just wanted to do it.

So, when we arrived at the appointed place, I stripped down to my trunks and jumped into the frigid water. When I emerged, the ship's doctor and his assistant were waiting with towels and my three layers of warm clothing. The chilly dip earned me a certificate, signed by two witnesses, that I was an official member of the Antarctic Polar Plunge Club.

The day after that memorable "swim," we spent three hours in a small boat visiting a place called "The Iceberg Graveyard."

This fascinating place featured icebergs of different colors, large and small. Some were as big as a factory building.

And they were slowly melting.

The day after cruising among icebergs, on January 22, 2010, we went ashore one last time. For this expedition, we received certificates stating that we had set foot on the continent of Antarctica at this particular place and at this point in time.

I received a second certificate, signed by the ship's captain and the expedition leader: This document certified that I was the oldest known person who had set foot on the continent.

It was time to begin the long journey back to North Carolina, which meant crossing the Drake Passage once again.

This warm body of water, between the southern tip of South America and Antarctica's South Shetland Islands, connects the southwestern part of the Atlantic Ocean with the southeastern part of the Pacific Ocean.

The commingling of water currents of different temperatures creates a turbulent sea, but, armed with knowledge from my first crossing, I fared much better on the return trip.

I said goodbye in Ushuaia to the vessel that had carried me to Antarctica. It had been a once-in-a-lifetime experience with a group of adventurers from fourteen countries around the globe.

These were hardy folks who enjoyed the challenge of coping with the forces of nature. One group had spent a night on shore in tents. Another paddled amid ice floes in kayaks. Most were between forty and sixty years of age. There were a few younger, a few older.

Many were professionals who worked with computers in some fashion. I made many friends among the group and as our days together were winding down many said they wanted to exchange email addresses so we could stay in touch.

I told them I did not own a computer, but that when I got home I would buy one and be in touch. And I did. I have been corresponding with several of my fellow Antarctic explorers ever since.

Antarctica is like no other place on earth. It is the coldest place on the planet, an environment harsh and forbidding for people.

It was a grand experience for me to see another example of God's creation and to ponder its role in nature.

I would not care to see this place again, but I am thankful I had the opportunity to see it once.

*If you're trying to accomplish something, the greater you're trying to accomplish, the bigger the risk.*

# A Flight of Honor

IN MAY 2010, I was selected, as a World War II veteran, to participate in a Triad Flight of Honor to Washington, D.C., to visit the World War II Memorial and other memorials in the nation's capital.

A hundred World War II vets, including three from my home county of Randolph—Archie Smith, Joseph Thomas, and me—were on the flight, along with their guardians.

Our guardian was Trent Thomas, the son of Wayne Thomas, who was the group leader. We left from the Piedmont Triad International Airport in Greensboro at 8:30 in the morning. Motor coaches carried us from the Reagan National Airport to the World War II Memorial.

The memorial covers several acres. There are fountains and a monument for each state. Other monuments are dedicated to Pearl Harbor and other important events during the war. It took a long time to see it all.

We moved on to the Vietnam Veterans Memorial. As I walked along the wall reading the names of those who lost their lives in this senseless, unnecessary and unpopular war, I was humbled and saddened. To me, this war should never have happened.

Next we visited the Lincoln Memorial, which honors a man whom I consider was inspired by divine guidance in providing the leadership demanded during the greatest crisis in our nation's history.

A chiseled wreath adorns a monument at the Korean War Veterans Memorial. Inside the wreath are these words: Uncommon Valor Was A Common Virtue.

Harry Truman, a man I have always admired, was president during the Korean War. He was a common man with an uncommon ability to figure out what was going on.

The most inspiring monument I saw was the one depicting the raising of the flag on Iwo Jima.

We visited Arlington National Cemetery, which I had visited many times before. As the years have passed, it has continued to expand and will do so in the future.

We also visited the Navy Log Room (one of our Randolph County veterans, Archie Smith, was a Navy man). We also stopped at the United States Air Force Memorial and then rode past the U.S. Capitol and the Washington Monument on the way back to the airport.

We arrived back in Greensboro at 8:00 p.m. and were greeted by a throng of people lined along the airport concourse. They cheered and thanked us for our service to our country.

I know I am like others who made the trip in appreciation of the opportunity, a trip I will cherish as long as I live.

# What's Next?

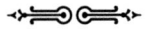

A footnote about my thoughts while visiting Arlington National Cemetery: These words, written by Father Denis Edward O'Brien (USMC), come to me when I visit a cemetery where veterans are buried. I read them in a newspaper many years ago. They are seared into my memory.

> *It was the veteran, not the reporter,*
> *who has given us freedom of the press.*
> *It was a veteran, not the poet,*
> *who has given us freedom of speech.*
> *It was the veteran, not the lawyer,*
> *who has given us the right to a fair trial.*
> *It was a veteran, not the campus organizer,*
> *who has given us freedom to demonstrate.*
> *It is the veteran who salutes the flag,*
> *who served under the flag,*
> *and whose coffin is draped by the flag,*
> *who allows the protester to burn the flag.*

All gave some.
Some gave all.

*We were created to move. Exercise even if you don't feel like it. Exercise even when it hurts.*

# On the Dance Floor in Maui

I WAS NINETY-SEVEN when I took my first trip to Hawaii in 2011.

One of my great-grandsons was getting married on January 16 on the island of Maui.

My invitation had arrived months in advance and I knew that I planned to attend. I also knew that a wedding in Hawaii would involve dancing, a lot of dancing, and I wanted to be able to join in the fun.

The problem was that I did not know how to dance.

The solution was to learn.

So, I signed up to take ballroom dancing lessons. For three months prior to the wedding, from October through December, I drove the 35 miles to the city of Greensboro two nights a week for dance class. I did not tell any of my family or friends what I was doing.

A travel agency handled my travel arrangements. The day before my scheduled departure, an 8:00 a.m. flight leaving from the Greensboro airport, a huge winter storm dumped snow and ice in the area.

Whenever I flew out of Greensboro, my habit was to drive to a hotel at the airport the day before my flight, spend the night and leave my car in the hotel parking lot. On this occasion, a mixture of snow and sleet was falling when it was time for me to head for the hotel.

My flight from Greensboro would take me to Atlanta and then on to Hawaii. Due to the storm, the Atlanta airport had already closed. As I was preparing to head out the door for Greensboro, my oldest son called.

"You aren't going, are you?" he asked.

"Yes," I replied. "It might be better in the morning."

I checked with my travel agency and was told that people were still traveling the highways and that the Greensboro airport was still open. I made the trip with no difficulties, checked in at the hotel and called my son to let him know I was safe.

The following morning, I checked out of the hotel at 4:00 a.m. to go to the airport. When I arrived there, I learned that my 8:00 a.m. flight was still on, but that there was also a flight bound for Atlanta at six with seats available. I caught the earlier plane and arrived in time for breakfast.

Due to the weather, my non-stop flight to Honolulu had been delayed for two hours. I had not had time to call my son before leaving Greensboro, so I called him after arriving in Atlanta. He was surprised to hear where I was and that I would be bound for Hawaii in the early afternoon.

As it turned out, we were delayed in Atlanta even longer than two hours while the plane was deiced but we finally got in the air. We encountered weather, and another delay, in Hawaii. This time the culprit was a violent thunderstorm.

By the time we landed and I had made a very long walk through the airport to catch a small commuter plane for the final leg of the journey—a thirty-five-minute flight to Maui—I had missed that flight. The next one was not leaving for more than an hour.

It was raining when we finally boarded the small plane. There were just a few of us on board, including an elderly couple and a group of teenage boys and girls.

My flight companions were local people and did not seem much concerned by the thunder, lightning, and rain, even though the plane bounced about as we plowed ahead through the storm. I had been a licensed pilot for twenty-five years, but I had never flown in that kind of weather. Still, I decided if it did not bother my fellow passengers, I was not going to let it bother me.

We arrived at Maui forty minutes after we took off, but it seemed to me like we had been in the air much longer than that. A taxi took me the final twenty miles through pouring rain.

My grandson Ronnie, the father of the groom-to-be, was staying at the same hotel. He helped me carry my bags to my room.

It had been a very long day, but I was in Maui, which is called "the magic isle."

Since I had time to explore the beautiful island, I stayed busy doing just that. One excursion found me taking a bus to the top of an extinct volcano more than 10,000 feet tall. On the summit I saw a huge crater blasted out long, long ago.

The tour guide said that Mark Twain had visited the volcano a hundred years earlier on horseback. I wondered how long it had taken to ride from the valley floor.

Maui boasts beaches lined with world-class resort facilities; outstanding golf courses that offer spectacular views of the blue waters of the Pacific Ocean; dramatic geography from the sea to mountains; and small-town charm.

Something that surprised me as I toured the island was that I saw no small farms. In the valley, I visited a huge sugar plantation of more than five thousand acres. The entire acreage was irrigated using water collected in the mountains and delivered down the mountainside, through the rainforest, and to the valley via canals dug by Chinese laborers a century earlier. A sugar mill on the plantation converted sugar cane syrup into raw crystalline sugar.

Another outing found me touring the rainforests and the coast. Between them, on the land sloping up toward the mountains, were large cattle ranches with plenty of grass and other vegetation for the animals.

I toured Haleakala National Park, which, at its highest point, rises more than 10,000 feet above sea level to the summit of a dormant volcano. The flanks of the mountain descend all the way to the sea. It is the island's most visible landmark.

The wedding was held in a small stone church that had been built by missionaries.

Before entering the church, visitors must remove their shoes. This was something I had never experienced before, and it was the first wedding I had ever participated in without my shoes.

The bride's grandfather had a large home on Maui. After the ceremony, we went to his house for a wedding dinner.

When the meal was done, the tables were cleared from the floor: It was time to dance.

The young people congregated on the dance floor, while we older folks took to the seats arranged around the walls. I sat between the host of the party and my grandson Ronnie.

After watching the youngsters dance for a while, some of the older women got up and started looking for dance partners among the men glued to chairs around the room.

This was the moment I had been waiting for. When the first lady asked me to dance, I got out of my chair and started living my dream: I was dancing in Hawaii.

I put my dance lessons to good use with four women and then with the bride. Needless to say, everyone was flabbergasted to see this ninety-seven-year-old man on the floor. I even received a round of applause.

From beginning to end, my Hawaiian trip was out of the ordinary. In fact, I would classify it as an extraordinary trip of adventure that I enjoyed and will always remember.

*At this point in my life, I'm not really afraid of anything.*

# A Minor Bump in the Road

THE IMMEDIATE EUPHORIA of my Pacific island jaunt was short-lived. The day after I arrived back home, I had an attack of diverticulitis and wound up in the emergency room.

My suspicion is that the attack came about because of the food I ate on the long flight home. I eat a special diet to stave off attacks of diverticulitis, a fare what was not available on the airplane.

I was hospitalized for four days, during which I received a blood transfusion and treatment to stop the bleeding. I was X-rayed and scanned. The tests revealed a large growth on my right kidney.

A specialist told me I had two options—treat the growth with medicine or have the kidney removed. I decided to have the surgery.

When I went to the hospital in Winston-Salem to consult with the surgeon, however, he advised me that he could do the operation, but that at my age the removal of one kidney could cause the other one to shut down.

Without hesitation, I canceled the surgery.

As far as I knew, the growth was not malignant and was not causing me any trouble. I had no intention of getting into a long, painful and costly medical treatment that might have disastrous effects.

I would wait and face any problems in the future, if any problems ever occurred.

*I have a high respect for responsibility.*

# Remembering North Carolina Veterans

EARLY IN 2011, members of the Randolph County Board of Commissioners chose five living veterans from the county to represent Randolph in the North Carolina Veterans Park, which was under construction in Fayetteville, near Fort Bragg.

One feature of the park would be a wall on which a hundred bronze casts were mounted—casts created from molds of the right hand of a veteran from each of the state's one hundred counties.

It was an honor and a privilege for all of us to be chosen. As the oldest veteran from Randolph, I was selected to have a mold made of my hand.

When I appeared before county commissioners to thank them for the honor, I told them I wanted them to know that I was a descendant of James Pugh, a Regulator who fought the British soldiers of King George in the Battle of Alamance in Orange County, North Carolina. He was caught after the battle and hanged at the courthouse in Hillsboro, near the present-day town of Chapel Hill.

It is a matter of record that he personally dispatched a number of British soldiers with his rifle. He gave his life at an early age in the fight for freedom. I told the commissioners that I was proud to be a descendant of James Pugh.

I have read all of the history I can find of veterans in our county from the days of my ancestor until now in the continuing battle for freedom. In my opinion, the North Carolina Veterans Park is another step in remembering our veterans – lest we forget.

I was privileged and honored to attend and participate in the dedication of the park along with family, friends, fellow veterans and many other people who were there that day.

*My life is ending. My worldly knowledge has not prepared me for transfer to another world. It's only my faith.*

# A Nightmare of Infections

AT ABOUT THREE o'clock in the morning on January 6, 2012, I experienced a very bad attack of diverticulitis—my ninth since I turned eighty-one.

The hospital was five miles from my house and I was afraid to try to drive myself, so I called my son Richard. He lived a few miles from me.

By the time he arrived at my house, I was bleeding badly. On the way to the emergency room, I lost consciousness (for only the second time in my life). I never even knew when we arrived. When I woke up, I was in a bed with staff attending to me. They told me I had lost a considerable amount of blood—my jeans had been so blood-soaked they'd had to cut them off of me—and needed a transfusion.

The bleeding stopped after I had been hospitalized for a few days and I was on the verge of going home. Then they discovered that I had a staph infection.

Before I knew it, I was seriously ill.

Some days, I did not know where I was or what was going on.

Some days, the doctor was not sure I would survive.

There were days and nights when I walked in the valley of death. I do not recall how many days I spent in this condition, but I survived.

Since I was going to need further treatment—antibiotics and other medications for another forty-five days—it was decided to transfer me to a nursing facility in Asheboro. Two days after I moved in, my left knee became infected with yet another virus, requiring immediate surgery. So, back to the hospital I went.

After the operation and an overnight stay, it was back to the nursing home where I began receiving treatment for two infections. What I experienced during the early days of this regimen seems almost unbelievable now.

Every day, I was receiving antibiotics via an IV inserted in the bicep muscle of my right arm. I also was taking an assortment of medications by mouth.

The effects of the infections were dramatic.

The nights were worst.

My body slept, but my mind did not. It worked overtime.

In dreams during my fitful slumber, I was a traveler in a foreign land—a strange place among strange people. I could not understand their language and I was being moved about in a wheelchair with no idea where I was going or why.

I asked why I was there and when I could go home.

Some days were no better.

Awake in my room at the facility, I wondered not only where I was but also why I was there. When I asked, a nurse would explain everything to me and I would not believe her.

One morning I was seated in a wheelchair and a nurse brought me breakfast. I refused to eat unless she told me where I was and why I was there. She told me. And I told her she was not telling me the truth.

At that moment, my son Richard walked into the room. I recognized him and suddenly realized that she had been telling me the truth. I immediately apologized.

Why was my brain doing this to me? Was illness affecting my brain? Or did the drugs cause my confusion?

I had heard of people on drugs and how it affects the mind. Now I know firsthand.

The strange thing about all of this is that while my physical body was inactive, my mind was busy recording all of this so I would know later what had been happing. It has become a part of my memory bank.

As the days passed, the drugs did their job. I gained strength and the infections diminished. I was about halfway through the treatment process and still taking the same amount of medication, but my mind was no longer running wild. My brain returned to normal—no more nightmares and delusions.

After forty-five days, the antibiotic had completed its work: It had destroyed every germ, bad and good, in my body, leaving my natural immune system in a shambles. The infections were gone, but so were my strength and energy.

When I was discharged from the nursing home, I was in no condition to return home and live by myself. After discussing the situation with my son Richard, who is my power of attorney, we decided that I would take an apartment at Clapp's Mountain Top Living in Asheboro. He lives just three miles from this facility, which is near the hospital, doctors' offices, drug stores, the grocery store and any other facilities I might want (or need to) visit, including the Randolph-Asheboro YMCA.

Of course, I was not able to help move furniture or do much of anything to help prepare my apartment. Richard and his wife, Betty, put in many hours of hard work getting my new home ready.

I could not yet drive again, so Richard had to take me on all my visits to the hospital and to see doctors—and there were many. But after a few weeks, the doctor said I had gained enough strength to take to the wheel again.

Richard handed over the keys to my car. I did not know it then, but I would be spending a lot of time in the coming months driving to and from the hospital and doctors' offices and the drug store.

I am grateful to the doctors and nurses at Randolph Hospital for the professional care I received. It was as good—or better—than I might have received somewhere else. I am sure that they saved my life. I am also thankful for the high-quality care I received from Clapp's Convalescent Nursing Home.

Thanks to them all, I was on the road to complete recovery, but still I faced a struggle to regain my previous stamina and return to my former state of fitness. I had no idea how long that journey was going to be.

But life goes on.

You have to keep trying.

*I'm slowly reaching the end of my rope,
but I'm still enjoying doing it—or trying to do it.*

## Back in the Games

I MOVED INTO my new apartment on April 12, 2012.

Two days later, I entered the annual Randolph County Senior Games.

I was not really in any condition to compete, but to achieve my goal of participating in the state games the following September, I had to qualify via the local games.

I was still using a cane to help me get around. During the local games, I would lay the cane on the ground, take my turn, pick the cane back up and walk to the next event. In this fashion, I qualified for the state games in four events—discus, shot put, horseshoes and shuffleboard.

By summertime, I had managed to discard the cane but was not regaining strength as quickly as I had hoped. That July, I discovered that I was passing a small amount of blood through my intestines. I visited my doctor and told him I did not think it was a bout of diverticulitis.

He inserted a light and camera into my stomach and found a bleeding vein, which he was able to repair. The loss of blood had lowered my blood count to 9.9 (14 is normal), which resulted in anemia and a loss of energy.

The doctor prescribed iron tablets and my blood count gradually rose to 11.3—still low, but better.

When September rolled round, I was determined to go to Raleigh, the site of the state games some 65 miles from my home. I enlisted the help of friends to drive me to the competition. I figured if someone could drive me there and drop me off close to the site of each I could walk a short distance, saving my energy to throw the shot put (or whatever) and take part in the competition.

So, that is what I did.

Thanks to the assistance of friends, I qualified for the National Games in Cleveland, Ohio, in July 2013.

*You're only going to live so many days. The important thing is the quality of the days, not the length.*

# Ditching the Drugs

I ACHIEVED MY goals for 2012 when I gained entry to the National Senior Games. I had goals for 2013 too.

My first goal was to attend and participate in the Games. The second major goal on my list was to have a big celebration of all my family and friends on October 12, 2013, my one hundredth birthday.

But to back up a bit: My health on my 99th birthday was not good. My blood count was low; I was anemic; and I had little strength or energy.

I was still recuperating from the weeks in the hospital and nursing home and was still under the supervision of doctors. And I was still taking lots of medications.

On October 25, less than two weeks after my ninety-ninth birthday, I awakened early in the morning and realized that I was experiencing the symptoms of a stroke. I called my son Richard and asked him to come take me to the emergency room.

I was in the hospital for several days while they ran tests to figure out what was going on. The doctors determined that I had had a minor stroke, which affected the right side of my face and head. They prescribed a number of medications: a blood thinner; iron capsules; a sinus spray; and various pills for my stomach, to manage my cholesterol and to treat constipation.

They told me that as long as I took the iron pills, I would have to take the constipation pills. I was also told that the blood thinner might trigger an attack of diverticulitis and internal bleeding.

When I was dismissed from the hospital I had the prescriptions filled and started taking all those pills.

My doctor issued other orders, too. He told me to stop going to the YMCA weekly to lift weights. He restricted my activity to walking.

The effects of the stroke, combined with taking all those drugs, left me weak and stressed. Then I became depressed. Some days I felt like I wanted to just close my eyes and go to sleep and never wake up.

My spirit came to my rescue.

I took the medicines as prescribed. I ate regularly, though I was not hungry, because I knew I needed to eat to survive. And I took regular walks because I knew I needed some kind of exercise.

October, November, and December passed. On New Year's Day 2013, after more than two months on the medications, the only improvement in my condition of which I was aware was an increase in my blood count. I knew that because I had to have it checked every few weeks.

Otherwise, my physical condition was a disaster. I lacked any strength. My energy had disappeared.

I had spent the entire year taking an assortment of drugs under the care of various physicians and had spent an inordinate amount of time in the hospital, in the nursing home and in doctors' offices.

When I rang in 2013, my condition was worse than when I rang in 2012. I sought solutions to my health woes, but despite all the medical advice had found none.

I had two goals for the year. One was to participate in the National Senior Games in Cleveland, Ohio, in July. The other was to throw a large birthday party in October, inviting all my family and friends to help me celebrate my one hundred years of inspired living on this earth.

My health at the beginning of the year was not promising: I was recovering from a minor stroke, had a large growth covering my right kidney, and was taking a lot of medications.

I had little strength or energy and was subject to attacks of internal bleeding, or another stroke.

But life goes on.

The best thing I had going for me was strength of spirit, which gave me hope that I would be able to find the path to achieve my goals in my ninety-ninth year.

When I suffered an attack of diverticulitis on January 5, I called my son Richard to take me to the hospital. Fortunately, it was a mild attack and the bleeding stopped on its own. This had never happened during my previous attacks and it turned out to be a good omen. After a couple of days in the hospital, I was able to return home.

One of the medications I had been taking was a blood thinner. In my opinion, it had been the cause of my internal bleeding. I stopped taking it. Another prescription was for iron tablets to build up my blood. To me, this seemed to be the only medication that was really working.

When I had finished the one hundred-pill prescription of iron, the doctor ordered a lab test to check my blood. The test showed that the iron tablets had done their job. He took me off the iron pills and the constipation pills I was taking because I was on the iron pills. I decided to quit taking all of the other medications I'd been prescribed for this or that ailment in the past year, too.

In a few days, I started feeling better.

In a few weeks, I felt the best I had in more than a year.

*To be part of something at any age is really rewarding to me. I try to get some enjoyment out of everything I'm involved in.*

## The Games Beckon

SOON I WAS back at the YMCA three days a week, exercising and lifting weights, building strength for the games in July.

I had already registered, had a hotel room reserved and a plane ticket to and from Cleveland.

I did not know if I would be in any condition to make the trip when the time rolled round, but I believed that if I tried, I would be able to go, participate and enjoy meeting old friends and making new ones.

It is exciting to be a participant in the largest group of elderly athletes ever assembled for competition. And there is plenty to do besides competing: parades, fireworks, and a host of entertainment of all kinds.

You have the opportunity to share the sights and sounds of each occasion with friends old and new to create memories that will last forever.

And you can say to each other, "We are never too old to have fun."

A month after I stopped taking any prescription medications, and with two months left before the senior games kicked off on July 19, my YMCA workouts were building my strength and stamina. I was also practicing pitching horseshoes and throwing the discus and the shot put. Rainy days prevented me from practicing outside as much as I would have liked, but I did what I could.

On July 18, I packed, climbed in my car, and drove the sixty-five miles to the airport near Raleigh. I spent the night in a nearby hotel. The next morning, I left my car at the hotel and took a shuttle bus to the terminal where I boarded my flight bound for Cleveland.

All of the seats on the fifty-passenger jet were filled and there was just one flight attendant. She was very busy. She appeared much older than the average flight attendant.

I had a chance to talk with her briefly and learned that her name was Beth. She was charming. She was 58 and had been a flight attendant for twenty years. She did not look that old.

As I was getting off the plane in Cleveland, she pinned a small set of silver wings onto my jacket. We had been strangers about two hours earlier. Now we were like neighbors who had shared a few moments of our lives together.

I was the last passenger to leave the plane. The captain was standing in the doorway to the cockpit as I approached the exit. Beth had told him that I was on my way to the senior games as a participant in the one hundred-year-old category.

He asked if he could have his picture made with me. I asked if he would send me a copy and gave him my address.

*It's been a rewarding trip. I've met a lot of people, made a lot of friends, and won a lot of medals.*

## At The Games

I UNPACKED MY bags and settled in for a brief rest at the Cleveland Sheraton before a prearranged meeting that afternoon with a reporter from the Greater Cleveland Sports Commission.

The interview lasted an hour. Then I headed downtown for the opening ceremonies of the Games. First I had to take a train, then a trolley to get to a pedestrian mall near the convention center.

Due to my hearing disability, I could not understand the conductor when the train stops were announced, so I used a map to follow our progress. When we arrived at the ninth stop, my destination, I got off and took an escalator from the underground station to the street and walked a short distance to a trolley stop.

I found a large crowd assembled in front of a stage at the mall, where loud rock music blared. Susan Strayhorn, a woman from Asheboro with an interest in the senior games, had driven to Cleveland.

We watched the opening ceremonies together, including the arrival of the torch, other festivities and then a large fireworks display. We returned to the hotel, where she was staying, too, and said goodnight. The next morning, a Saturday, we returned downtown to The Village, the headquarters for the Games. It occupied an entire floor of the convention center.

When I checked in a young woman at the desk acted surprised when I gave her my name and address. She asked me to have a seat and said there was someone who wanted to meet me.

A few minutes later another young woman walked up and introduced herself. Her name was Meredith Scerba. She was senior vice president of the Greater Cleveland Sports Commission and executive director of the National Senior Games.

She told me that she had been born in Pinehurst, North Carolina, which is just a few miles south of where I live, and that her mother lives in Greensboro, a few miles north.

An outstanding swimmer, she had attended college in Ohio on scholarship. That's where she met her future husband. She gave me her card and her cell phone number and told me if I had any problems to give her a call.

I saw her several times during the Games as she made her rounds. She always stopped to chat for a few minutes. One night she invited me to dinner with three interns on her staff.

The last time I saw her, on the last day of the Games, she was checking on cleanup efforts in the gyms. I would characterize her as a charming and gracious young lady.

Maybe in the course of events I will have the pleasure of meeting and talking with her again.

*There's no way you can overcome age,
no matter how much you practice.*

# Bringing Home
# The Gold

When I checked in as an athlete, I received a schedule with the day, time and location of my three events and instructions on using the transit system to get from place to place.

Cleveland is a large city and event venues were scattered over a wide area for the 11,000 expected participants.

My first event—horseshoes—was set for Wednesday. As I waited for my turn, I sat with friends and family members watching the competition and chatted with three women seated next to me. The two to my right were from Texas; the one to my left was from Virginia.

We talked about our families, our homes, and our experiences getting to and getting around Cleveland. We shared anecdotes and jokes. We clapped and cheered when a family member was competing. We were no longer strangers, but friends enjoying each other's company.

Then it was my turn.

As it turned out, no one else had registered in the one hundred-year-old category meaning that I was an automatic gold-medal winner—after I proved that I could play the game.

I competed against three athletes in the ninety-year-old division. I played three games and won one. I had earned my first gold medal of the 2013 Games.

The following day, I was scheduled to throw the discus. While I was waiting for the event to begin, I received a special surprise: Ruth and Kathryn Pugh, my grandson's wife and their oldest daughter, came walking up. They had driven from Asheboro to see me participate.

I was delighted to see them and ready to compete. I had been lifting weights for three months, building strength and stamina. Having Ruth and Kathryn there as spectators gave me extra incentive to do my best.

I made six throws, one good enough to set a world record for the discus in the one hundred-year-old age group, and earned my second gold medal of the Games.

Ruth, Kathryn, my Asheboro friend Susan Strayhorn, and I celebrated by going out to dinner.

The next day was my shot put event. My competitor was a man from South Dakota who had beat me by five inches in the national games four years earlier. This time was my turn on top of the podium. I took home the gold; he got the silver.

Once again, the four of us marked the occasion with dinner. The next day we took a cruise on the river that bisects the city. We had a lot of fun and took a lot of pictures.

*I wouldn't want to be a famous person.*
*I wouldn't want all my privacy taken away from me.*
*But it's nice to meet 'em if I meet 'em in the course of events.*

# A New Role Spectator

DURING MY FIRST seven days in Cleveland I met new people, made new friends and enjoyed dining out every night of the week.

Wherever we went, I wore two things: the ID card that identified me as a senior games participant and a light blue North Carolina Tar Heels ball cap. Both of these items, as well as my age, attracted attention.

We visited some restaurants a second time. When we did that, we were no longer strangers. I talked with waiters, waitresses and restaurant patrons. You can find out a lot about people by being interested in them and asking questions. Sometimes you learn more by being an interested listener.

During the second week in Cleveland, I planned to spend most of my time watching competition in basketball, volleyball and pickleball, which is a growing racquet sport.

I was especially interested in the basketball games because my friend Michael Hess, a board member of the National Senior Games Association, was chair of the basketball program. His headquarters in Cleveland was a large gym with four basketball courts at Cleveland State University. Next door was a gym with six courts.

I had a special chair next to Mike's desk. From that vantage point I could watch what was happening on the four courts. Usually, there were four games going on simultaneously.

Family and friends watched the games from chairs lined up around the walls of the gym, which was a beehive of activity.

There were 256 teams registered for the Games with competition going on in several locations around the city. You can imagine how many games had to be played to determine the winners.

I wore a gold medal around my neck and carried two in a shoulder bag. I was the only athlete in the gym with a medal. Many people approached me to get an up-close look at the medal and to have a picture made with me. I have no idea how many photographs were snapped while I was a basketball spectator.

But I recall one picture quite well.

One day four teams were playing. Mike came over and told me that Pat Boone, the pop singer who rivaled Elvis in popularity in the late 1950s and early 1960s, was a player on one of the teams. I went over to watch. Boone's team, the Virginia Creepers, was in the 75–79 age group.

When the game was over, I met him. We talked about my events and my gold medals. He told me that he had played basketball most of his life. He said he loved the game and that was why he was in the Games.

Boone was the starting point guard for his team. He knew how to play and his team was good, but they lost in the finals.

A photograph of Boone and me sharing a laugh was published in *The Cleveland Plain Dealer*.

Another player on the team had his picture made with me, too. He said he was going to put the photo in his local paper back home.

On another day I was watching a women's game pitting Carolina and Tennessee. A mother with two young children was sitting next to me. As we talked, I learned that the woman had a sister Tennessee's team. I met her after the game, which Tennessee won. They were happy and we said goodbye as new friends.

As the week went by, word got around that I was a triple gold medal winner. As I sat in the lobby that separated the two gyms eating popcorn, some people who spotted me on the bench would stop and ask if they could take a picture.

I only wore one medal in my travels. If I wore all three I sounded like a train coming when I walked. The picture takers always asked where my other two medals were and I would take them from my shoulder bag and drape them around my neck for the photo op.

Two very tall basketball players stopped one day and asked to pose with me. They were members of an Arkansas team in the 65–69 age group and invited me to come watch them play the next day. So I did.

Their team was tall and talented and they won the gold medal in their age bracket. After the championship game, they gathered for a group picture on the floor and asked me to join them. One of the players told me that when they got home to Arkansas, he was going to have the photo published in the local newspaper.

This was truly exciting stuff for me. I have a copy of the picture and will keep it.

Oh wow, what a combination—a tall, talented championship team and a triple gold medal-winning old man who is 5 feet 10 inches tall.

*Meeting and exchanging with people, creating friendships and memories. Good memories. You know, I can't think of a bad memory.*

## Goodbye to Cleveland

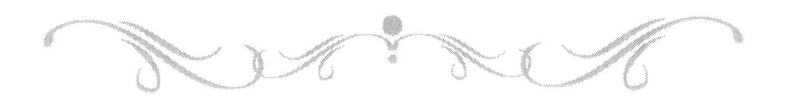

IT TAKES AN enormous effort by many people to prepare for an event that will host 11,000 athletes and more than 20,000 family members, friends and other spectators.

I watched the final games on the fourteenth—and last—day of the 2013 National Senior Games and then witnessed as a small army of staffers, interns and volunteers began cleaning up the gyms.

The Greater Cleveland Sports Commission had done an outstanding job recruiting and managing the large contingent needed to keep the Games on schedule, although without the interns and volunteers, it could not have happened.

I had found Cleveland to be a beautiful, clean, modern metropolis on Lake Erie. Its RTA transit system works well. During two weeks of traveling to and from events across the city I never had a problem.

Everyone involved in the 2013 games should be proud.

I had only a small part in the action, but I enjoyed it and am thankful for the privilege.

On my fifteenth day in Cleveland I checked out of my hotel to make my way to the airport to fly home. When I fly these days, I check in as a handicapped person and request a wheelchair.

I can walk, slowly, but given the rush of a busy terminal and the distance to get to departure gates and to board a plane, I am handicapped.

On the day I left Cleveland, I arrived at the gate with two hours to spare. I was sitting there alone in a wheelchair. A man walked up and asked about the gold medal around my neck.

I explained that I had two more gold medals and that I had earned them in the 100-year-old category of the senior games. He asked when my plane departed. When I told him, he asked me to come with him and meet some people.

He wheeled me to his office where I met several young women. I assumed they were members of his staff. They all wanted to have pictures made with me wearing my gold medals.

Then the man rolled me into a VIP lounge, settled me in a comfortable chair and gave me a newspaper. He said that he would return and roll me back to the gate in time for my flight.

And he did. I thanked him for his kindness and he handed me a business card. He was the operations manager for the airport. I had a new "email" friend in Cleveland.

The trip home was uneventful. My plane landed in Raleigh around noon; a shuttle bus delivered me to my car in the hotel parking lot; and I drove home, arriving at my apartment at about 3 o'clock.

I unpacked my baggage. It was mostly soiled garments, as I had done no laundry while I was gone. While I did laundry I checked my email, had dinner, and then sat down in my rocking chair to reflect on the past fifteen days.

I had experienced my most rewarding and enjoyable National Senior Games to date. I had met old friends and made far more new friends than ever before – and this included meeting and befriending more friends in the host city than I had anywhere else.

I enjoy competing in the games, but I get far more enjoyment in meeting, greeting and becoming friends with people from every corner of the United States of America.

You might be surprised at how many times we said to each other, when saying goodbye, "God bless you."

*Life's been a learning process. It still is. I'm still learning.*

# Back in the Groove

BACK HOME FROM the Games, I returned to a predictable schedule in the retirement facility where I live alone.

I prepare my own breakfast and lunch; dinners are prepared and served in the dining room. I do my own laundry and housekeeping.

On Mondays, Wednesdays and Fridays I go to the YMCA to lift weights for an hour.

And every morning at 8 o'clock, I call my oldest son to let him know that I am up and moving. If I am on a trip, I still call him at the same time on my cell phone. I have been doing this ever since my wife, Maxine, passed away.

She and I were always close to our children. In our busy lives, we always had time for them. We carried them to church regularly and on vacations often.

We were involved in their progress in school. We attended all of their school activities—band recitals, dance recitals, plays and ballgames. Sometimes both of us could not be on hand, but one of us was always there for them.

We always knew where they were and who they were with.

We taught them responsibility.

We have two sons; six grandsons; five great-grandsons; six great-granddaughters; two great-great-grandsons; and three great-great-granddaughters.

With just one or two exceptions, we have been present at every important event in each one of their lives.

In return our children have shown us love and respect.

Maxine passed away six years ago. Memories of her are part of daily life for me and for our children.

*Don't you want me to drive out on the highway
so you can see how fast I can go?*

# Good for Five More Years

MY DRIVER'S LICENSE was going to expire on my one hundredth birthday, so, a couple of weeks before that, on September 24, I drove to the state license office to apply for a new license.

I had prepared, brushing up on my knowledge of roadside signs and securing a document from my doctor stating that my eyesight was good enough to drive.

I passed the test in the office and was informed that I had to take a driving test. The woman who gave me the road test asked me to complete several driving maneuvers on several streets. She told me that I had passed the test.

I drove back to the drivers' license office where she gave me a new license good for five years. There are no restrictions on when or where I can drive until I am 105.

The license examiner told me she would not be afraid to drive with me anywhere. She made my day.

The next day, I drove forty miles to Greensboro to see my latest great-great-granddaughter, who was just over a month old. She was a beautiful baby. I held her for a few minutes and had pictures made. I visited with my great-grandson and his wife for a couple of hours. We said our goodbyes and they told me they would see me again on my birthday.

I drove home with pleasant thoughts for the company and the end of a perfect day.

*It's the party of a lifetime. I've never had a birthday party in my life to my knowledge.*

# A Century... and Counting

EARLY IN 2013, I set two goals. I achieved the first one when I was able to attend the senior games in Cleveland.

The time for the second one, October 12, my one hundredth birthday, was approaching.

I had planned to throw a party for myself, but learned that my local YMCA and my family were planning a party and celebration. They said all I had to do was show up.

On October 10, Debbie Carlisle, the manager of Clapp's Mountain Top Living, where I live, told me that she and the staff were having a birthday party for me too.

They decorated the facility's beautiful dining room with balloons and ribbons. I had a joyful time and enjoyed a delicious dinner with my fellow residents. They are friendly, caring and interested in each other.

The occasion is entered into my memory bank as a special one, in a special place, with special people.

As I had requested, the YMCA and my family invited all of my family, friends and neighbors to my birthday party on Saturday, October 12. To my surprise, the party turned out to be bigger than I expected.

I was honored with a letter of congratulations from my home city of Asheboro; a letter of acknowledgement from the North Carolina House of Representatives; and a letter of congratulations from the North Carolina governor. I was also awarded the Order of the Long Leaf Pine, which is one of the highest honors the governor can bestow on a resident of the Tar Heel state.

Hundreds of people attended the "celebration," which lasted about two hours. Everyone seemed to enjoy the occasion.

I was overwhelmed by the turnout. It was a testimony to the friendships and caring for each other that exist in our community.

That afternoon, a good friend invited me to go flying with him in his private plane, an aircraft once used as a training plane by the Swiss Air Force.

We took off from our local airport and flew around over the countryside, which is beautiful at that time of year. We were in a high-performance airplane with a sliding canopy and excellent visibility. I truly enjoyed this birthday present.

That evening, my oldest grandson and his wife, Ronnie and Teresa, hosted another birthday party in their home. This was a private affair for my family and me. The youngest member of the Pugh clan was Frances, the month-old daughter of Tyson and Collins Pugh.

My one hundredth birthday was a wonderful experience that ended with me surrounded by those I love beyond all others.

*I've been pretty confident about everything I've tried, even Dancing with the Stars.*

# Dancing With the Randolph Stars

I RECEIVED AN unexpected visit from Ann and Bill Hoover at my apartment in early January 2014.

The Hoovers, members of the planning committee for an event called Dancing with the Randolph Stars, delivered this message: Because you're a celebrity, the Randolph Community College Foundation needs you as a dancer for its fund-raiser.

"Are you serious?" I asked. "Do you know how old I am?"

I asked if they had given any thought to my mental and physical condition.

They didn't miss a beat: "Yes and we feel sure that you can do it."

Through the RCC Foundation, the annual Dancing with the Randolph Stars raises money for scholarships for students at RCC, the community college in Asheboro, where I live.

The Hoovers explained that there would be 18 couples. My dancing partner (who would be paired with me later) and I would receive three dancing lessons with a professional instructor.

We would pick our own music and the type of dance we wanted to do. We would be responsible for assembling our own costumes, for preparing for the dress rehearsal on May 30 and for the live performance the following evening.

I also would need to fill seats at one table with family and friends on the night of the show, and in the weeks and months before that encourage my family, friends, neighbors, even strangers, to vote (by making a cash donation) for my team.

I had only danced once in my lifetime. That was at the age of ninety-seven on the occasion of my great-grandson's wedding in Hawaii.

But I said yes.

Why not?

It was for a very good cause.

I met my partner, Linda Covington, on January 26. Lucky for me, she had been dancing since childhood and was an accomplished dancer.

She was gracious and helpful to me during our weekly practice sessions at the Randolph-Asheboro YMCA after we'd had our free lessons. Without Linda's outstanding assistance I would never have been able to give the performance I did a few months later.

For our routine, Linda and I chose to portray Ginger Rogers and Fred Astaire in a routine called "Stepping Out with my Baby." Linda would wear a beautiful dress; I would deck out in a tuxedo with tails, a white bow tie, a white vest, and a top hat.

On the night of dress rehearsal, I put on my fancy attire and headed down to dinner from my apartment at Clapp's

Mountain Top Living. My fellow residents had been very supportive of my dancing role and I had promised to show off my Fred Astaire persona.

I danced with some of the residents and posed for pictures. I enjoyed it and they did, too. Later, our dress rehearsal went very well.

The next night brought a sold-out house of fun-loving folks and eighteen couples ready to dance. Excitement and expectation filled the air.

Linda and I were the first to perform. Cheers greeted us as we stepped onto the stage and grew louder as we launched into our routine.

It was our crowd and the judges gave us a "10+."

We also received a standing ovation.

Every couple that followed gave outstanding performances and received cheers and applause. We gathered onstage when the dancing was done to receive trophies and awards. Most importantly, everyone was waiting to hear the announcement of how much money had been raised for scholarships.

The final tally was more than $200,000, which was $80,000 more than the previous year.

Dancing with the Randolph Stars was an outstanding success and I was privileged to be part of it.

I was fortunate to win an award, a trophy and praise for my participation.

But the most meaningful award arrived a week after the event in the form of a hand-written note: "Thank you, John," it read. "You stole the show and also my heart."

*I really have been a curiosity cat all my life. I wondered what, when and why did it happen? I still do.*

# My Search for Knowledge

AS FAR BACK as I can remember, I was filled with curiosity about the world around me. I wanted to know why, when and how things happened.

Even at an early age, I knew that I was having trouble understanding most of what I was hearing. I sensed that I was missing something but did not know what it was. I wanted to be understood and I wanted to participate in what was going on around me, but due to my hearing problem, it was not possible.

So, as a boy, I spent most of my time alone, roaming the woods and fields, fascinated by the birds, bees, snakes, ants and myriad other living creatures in nature's world.

Each busy being fulfilled its special role in life on earth.

Each shared the same beginning and end – born to live and to die.

I learned about the reality of life and death as a barefoot boy with nature as my teacher. It was the beginning of my lifelong search for knowledge, the meaning of knowledge and the value of knowledge.

As I grew older and entered my years of schooling, and then public employment, I acquired knowledge through experience and by reading good books. As I grew older and more involved in the responsibilities of life on earth, I realized the value of all sources of knowledge.

After I retired at the age of eighty-five, my continuing accumulation of knowledge helped me survive the problems of aging.

While I was reading about ancient civilizations in my early search for knowledge, I learned a couple of interesting things: One was that change was a constant factor in their lives; another was that they were constantly seeking to understand the world around them as well as to ponder their future.

I remember reading about a Chinese philosopher who lived some four thousand years ago and who wrote these words: It is a test of time to come to terms with change, to not be afraid of it, nor spend too much time in protest.

Throughout history, men have been seeking knowledge of the world and passing that knowledge on to the next generation. This process has resulted in a gradual increase in knowledge through the ages.

In the generations before I was born, the accomplishments of four men—Thomas Edison, Henry Ford, and Orville and Wilbur Wright—had astounding effects on the lives of their generation, and generations that followed, including mine. I have read biographies of all of them.

How did they accomplish the things that they did?

It was through trial and error over many hours, days, weeks, and, in some cases, years. They accumulated knowledge as they worked. Nothing came easy. Plain old staying with it enabled them to get the job done.

My generation sprang to life in the horse and buggy days, a humble beginning for a generation that has been called "The Greatest." But I have no doubt where the ability to accomplish all the things my generation has accomplished came from: It was from accumulated knowledge passed down from previous generations.

As I contemplate this fact, I am filled with awe and wonder at what future generations will be able to do, and, in fact, must do, to meet the problems of a constantly changing world.

They will need every bit of the accumulated knowledge added to their own acquired knowledge to find solutions to an array of challenges.

The earth's population is growing at an accelerated rate with each passing generation. The planet's resources to meet human needs are diminishing. Eventually, the human race will need more space. And it is available: on other planets in outer space, the new frontier. It is possible. It can happen and it will happen.

There have been those in the past who said it cannot be done.

And there have been those in the past who have gone out and done it.

There will be those in the future who will go out and do it.

Space travel has been accomplished in our generation. We are accumulating knowledge about space travel through trial and error, a process that has always worked.

The effort will require a tremendous amount of resources—money, materials, time, and human lives. But based on what the human race has accomplished in its past, if it has the spirit, the faith and the desire, man will travel to other planets.

Since I turned one hundred, a number of people have asked a similar question based on the fact that I have seen many changes during my long life: Is life on earth getting better or worse?

I answer without hesitation.

Without a doubt, it is getting better.

I have been a student of history all of my life. History shows us that throughout the centuries of civilization, man's lives have slowly but surely been getting better.

As amazing as it seems, I have witnessed more change in my lifetime affecting human life than occurred during the entire recorded history of man before me.

This is the result of accumulated knowledge.

Accumulated knowledge in the future will lead to life on earth improving even more.

There is one sobering fact to remember. Throughout man's history, there has been a war between good and evil. This war continues today. Who is winning? History says the good side. There are more good people on earth than evil people. This war of good versus evil is going on now and will continue until the final battle on earth—the battle of Armageddon—decides the winner.

My lifelong search for knowledge has been inspired by my spirit and motivated by my faith. I have dared to go where they led me. I have been inspired and motivated to create and to participate in my earthly life. My life story testifies to that fact.

In my search for knowledge, I have been taught the basic values of life on earth – love of God, love of family, love of friends, love of neighbors, love of community and love of country.

As I face life after one hundred years, I know my life on earth is coming to an end. I patiently wait for that time. I am in good health and to the best of my knowledge I am not afflicted with any terminal diseases.

I do some form of physical exercise every day except Sunday. Three days a week I "pump iron." I am not taking any kind of prescription medicine. I follow a diet that I developed through research, and trial and error, over the past twenty years in my struggle for survival. I also use some vitamins, herbs and supplements, a regimen that I also found through research, trial and error.

I live alone in a private apartment complex, comfortable and surrounded by friends. I still drive my car wherever I want to go. I frequently drive to visit family and friends wherever they live, regardless of the distance.

I have a computer room in my apartment. I use my computer frequently to exchange emails with family and friends around the world. Due to my age, I can no longer correspond via hand-written letters. But thanks to modern technology, I can dictate letters to my computer. My words are transferred to my printer. I mail letters to friends near and far and across the globe.

My memory is good. I always find things if I temporarily forget where I left something.

My life on earth has been a wonderful, exciting and rewarding journey. I have reached the point where I am like the twelve-year-old barefoot boy of long ago who leaned on a hoe in the tobacco field of his father's farm and looked skyward, mesmerized by a plane passing overhead.

Today, I gaze into the heavens with awe and wonder and ask myself: What's next?

And I humbly wait for the moment when my spirit will make the transition from my earthly body to the spirit world of my merciful heavenly Father.

John Pugh Jr. was working in a textile mill in 1943 when he volunteered to serve his country during World War II.

John met his future wife, Maxine Hill, on a blind date. They were married the same year. 'Don't take me long to make up my mind,' John says. 'Comes in pretty handy when you get in a close spot.'

## What's Next?

In 1939, John spent a year building a home. He pulled the night shift in a hosiery mill and worked on the house by day, buying materials as he needed them.

John hired a building contractor to build this service station, Pugh Esso, in rural North Carolina. The station opened in 1947. He kept his job in the mill, working both places, until he was satisfied he could earn a living in the new venture.

What's Next?

After taking flying lessons at the age of 44, John got a pilot's license. Among his flying ups and downs: He was forced to land his Piper Tri-Pacer in dense fog over Cape Cod in 1962.

John hired a grading contractor to build Pugh Field, a private landing strip, 100 feet wide and 2,000 feet long, behind his home. He's standing by his Piper Comanche on the grass airstrip.

John, who was 65 at the time, poses in the cockpit of his Piper Comanche. He flew off his private airstrip, for business and pleasure, for 25 years. He sold his plane and gave up flying at 70.

During a ten-day tour of Alaska with a group of North Carolina oil jobbers in 1974, John saw construction under way on the 800-mile Alaskan oil pipeline.

After 'retiring' from the oil business at the age of 70, John built a farm and went into the cattle-breeding business. That's him in the foreground of this picture, driving an Angus bull to the barn.

In 1994, at 81, John did something he had long dreamed of doing: rafting the Colorado River through the Grand Canyon. The adventure lasted eight days.

John and Maxine Pugh had been married for 73 years when she died on May 6, 2007, after several years of failing health. This was their last picture together before she got sick.

In June 2009, John set out on a ten-day excursion in the Canadian Rockies. One of his favorite memories of the trip: Riding a gondola traveling on a steel cable between two mountains, 7,486 feet up in the air.

What's Next?

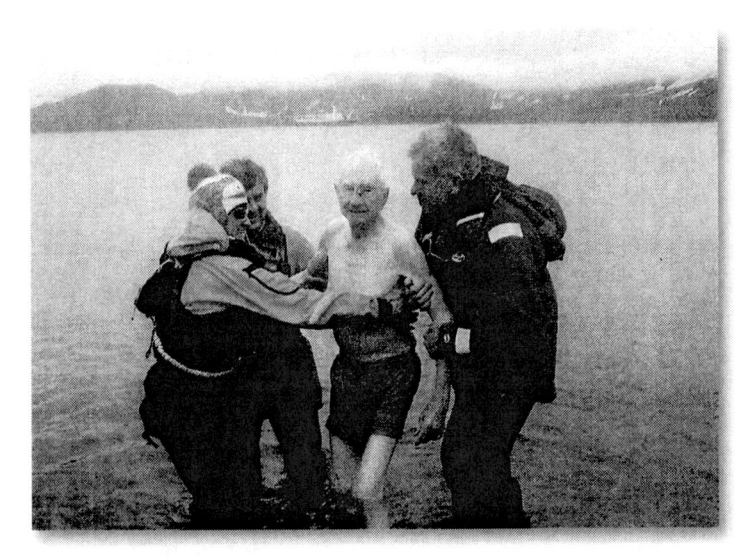

John was 96 when he booked voyage on an adventure ship bound for Antarctica. While there, he took 'the polar bear plunge' – jumping into the frigid waters – though the ship's doctor tried to talk him out of it.

John brought home three medals from the 2009 National Senior Games in California. He's posing with Martha Norman, left, and Hazel Anderson, two fellow residents of Asheboro, North Carolina, who also participated.

In May 2010, John took part in a Triad Flight of Honor to Washington, D.C., to visit the World War II Memorial. A trio of Randolph County vets posed at the memorial. Left to right are Archie Smith, John and Joseph Thomas.

John put on his dancing shoes in Maui, Hawaii, when one of his great-grandsons got married in 2011. Here he's dancing with the bride.

What's Next?

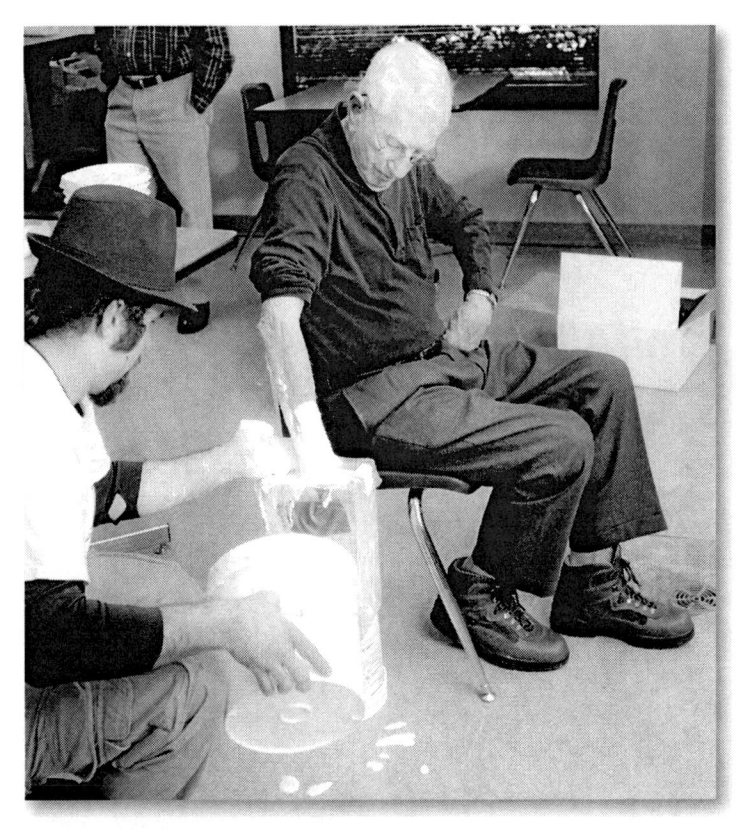

In 2011, Randolph County commissioners picked John – the oldest living veteran in the county – to have a bronze cast made of his hand for the North Carolina Veterans Park. (Photo courtesy The Courier-Tribune, Asheboro, N.C.).

John Pugh Jr. with Chip Womick

John stands at a wall which features 100 bronze hand casts – one from a veteran in every county in the state – during dedication of the North Carolina Veterans Park on July 4, 2011.

As a participant in the 100-year-old category, John won three gold medals at the 2013 National Senior Games in Cleveland, Ohio. (Photo courtesy The Courier-Tribune, Asheboro, N.C.)

John was 100 when he and his dancing partner Linda Covington wowed the crowd by portraying Ginger Rogers and Fred Astaire during a fundraising event called Dancing with the Randolph Stars. (Photo by Greg Stewart)

John and Linda Covington received a standing ovation (and trophies) after a routine called 'Stepping Out with my Baby' during Dancing with the Randolph Stars in May 2014.
(Photo by Greg Stewart)

CPSIA information can be obtained at www.ICGtesting.com
Printed in the USA
LVOW10s2040010415

432909LV00032B/1296/P

9 781630 639761